FRANKLIN PARK PUBLIC LIBRARY
FRANKLIN PARK, IL.

Each borrower is held responsible for all library material drawn on his card and for fines accruing on the same. No material will be issued until such fine has been paid.

All injuries to library material beyond reasonable wear and all losses shall be made good to the satisfaction of the Librarian.

Replacement costs will be billed after 42 days overdue.

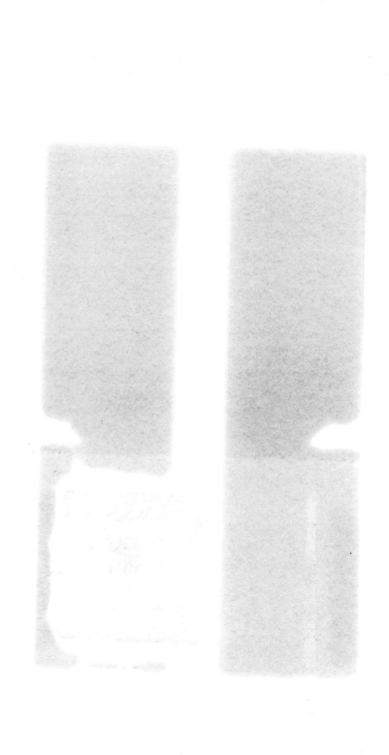

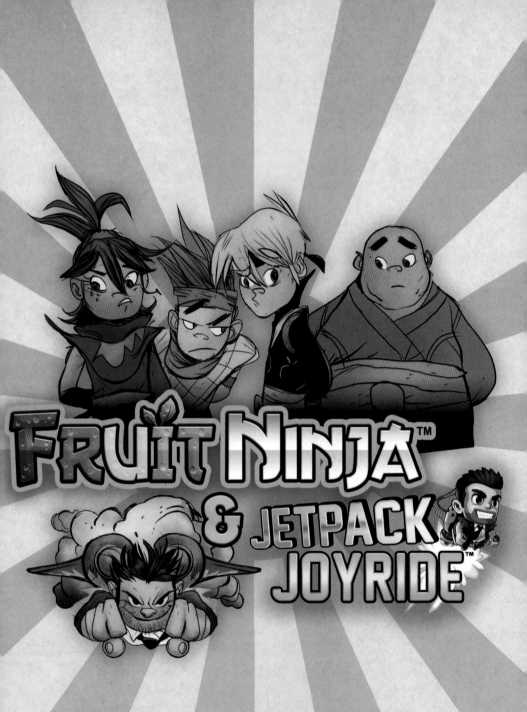

FRUIT NINJA™

& JETPACK
JOYRIDE™

DYNAMITE.

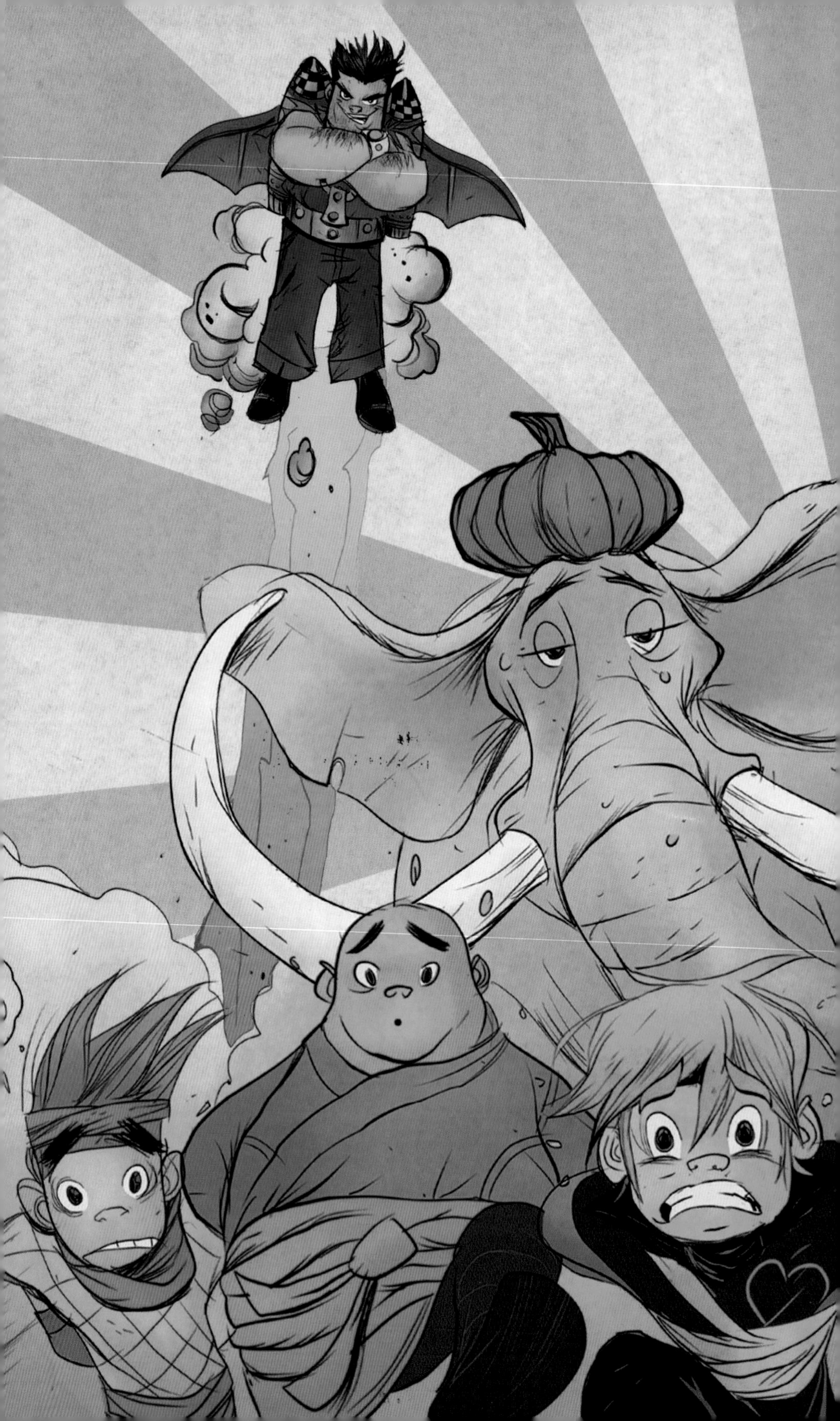

ANCIENT FRUIT NINJA

Art by Scott Brown

Color by Dearbhla Kelly

JETPACK JOYRIDE

Art by Scott Brown

Color by Dearbhla Kelly

MODERN FRUIT NINJA

Art by Ruairi Coleman & Sebastian Piriz

Color by Alfonso Espinoza,

Ellie Wright & Rebecca Nalty

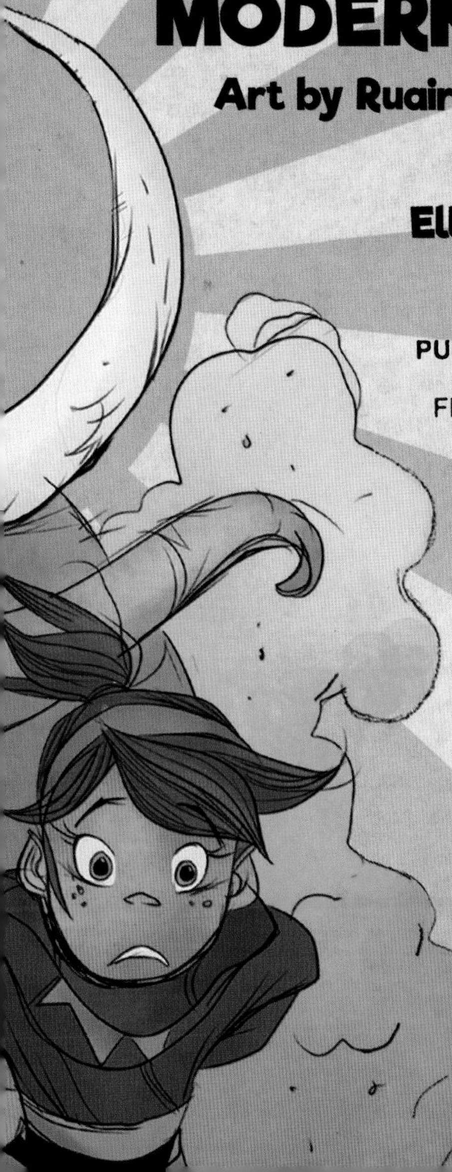

Letters by
Zakk Saam

Covers by
Scott Brown, with
Omi Remalante
& Dearbhla Kelly

Book Design by
Chris Mowry

Written, Packaged
& Edited by
Nate Cosby

Nick Barrucci CEO/Publisher
Juan Collado President/COO

Joseph Rybandt Executive Editor
Matt Idelson Senior Editor
Anthony Marques Associate Editor
Kevin Ketner Assistant Editor

Jason Ullmeyer Art Director
Geoff Harkins Senior Graphic Designer
Cathleen Heard Graphic Designer
Alexis Persson Graphic Designer
Chris Caniano Digital Associate
Rachel Kilbury Digital Multimedia Associate

Brandon Primavera V.P. of IT and Operations
Rich Young Director of Business Development

Alan Payne V.P. of Sales and Marketing
Pat O'Connell Sales Manager

J-GN
FRUIT NINJA
460-3901

ISBN:
978-1-5241-0573-0
First Printing
10 9 8 7 6 5 4 3 2 1
Printed in China

online **www.DYNAMITE.com**
Facebook /**Dynamitecomics**
Instagram /**Dynamitecomics**
Tumblr **dynamitecomics.tumblr.com**
Twitter **@dynamitecomics**

DYNAMITE.®

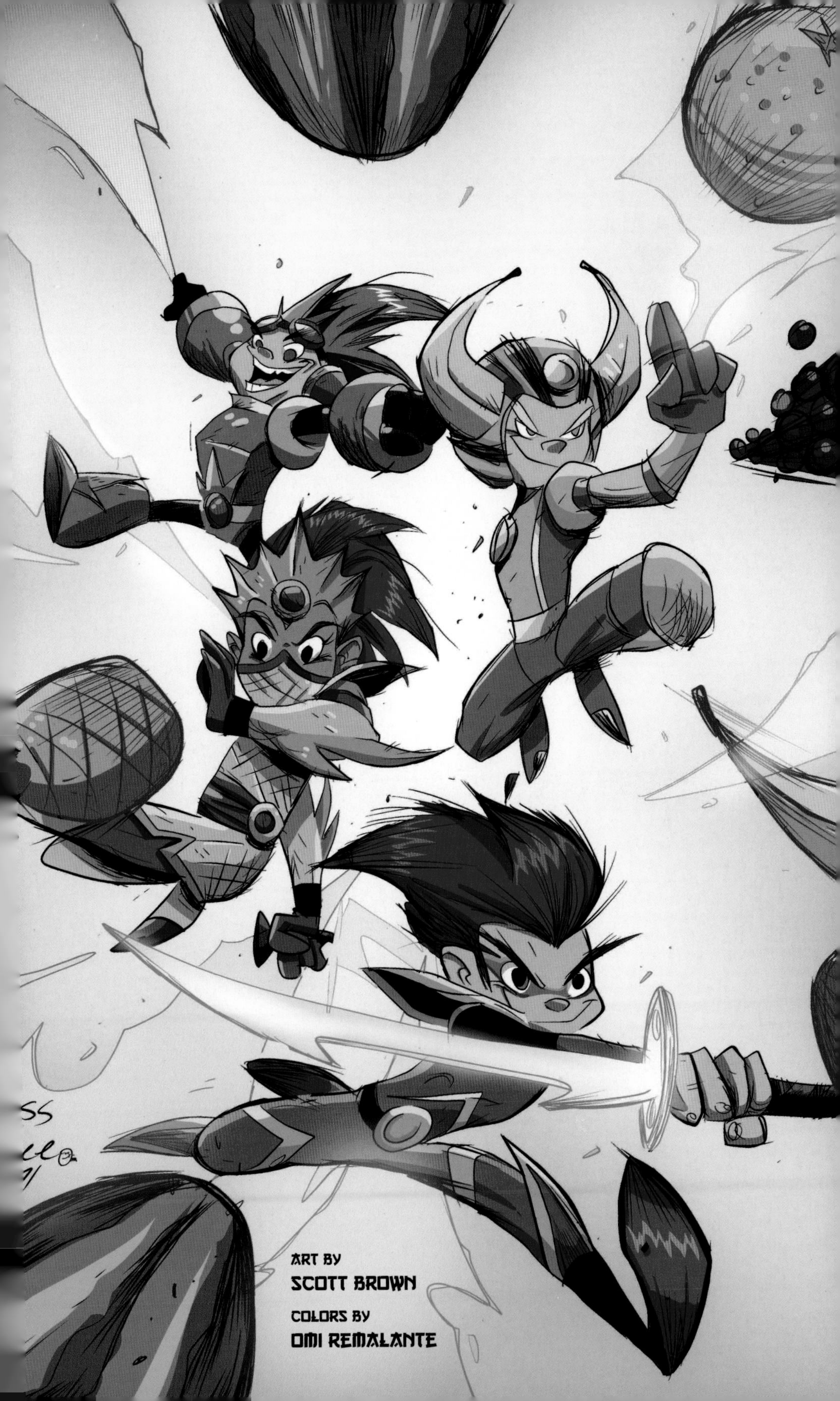
ART BY
SCOTT BROWN
COLORS BY
OMI REMALANTE

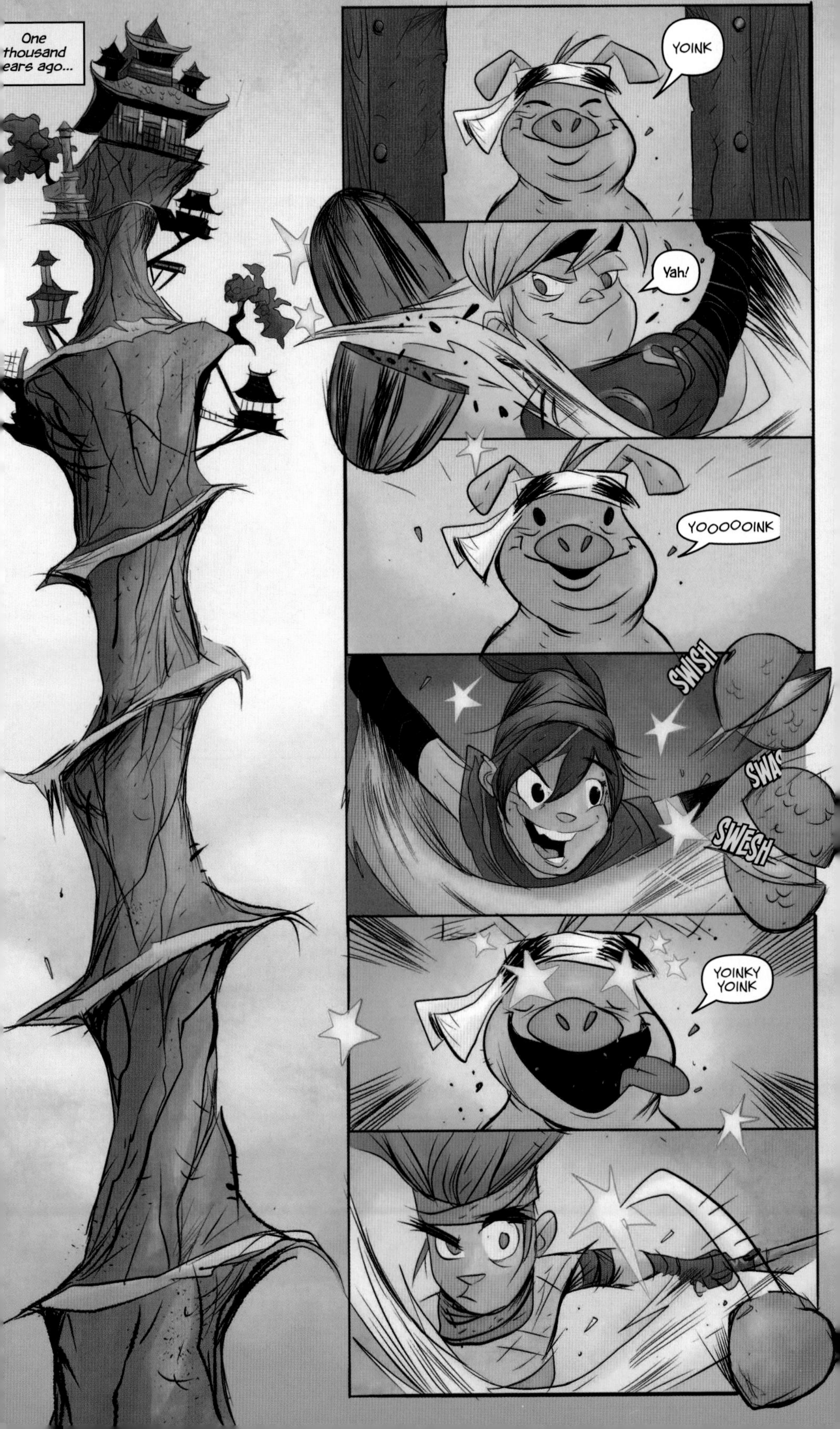
One thousand ears ago...
YOINK
Yah!
YOOOOOINK
SWISH
SWAS
SWESH
YOINKY YOINK

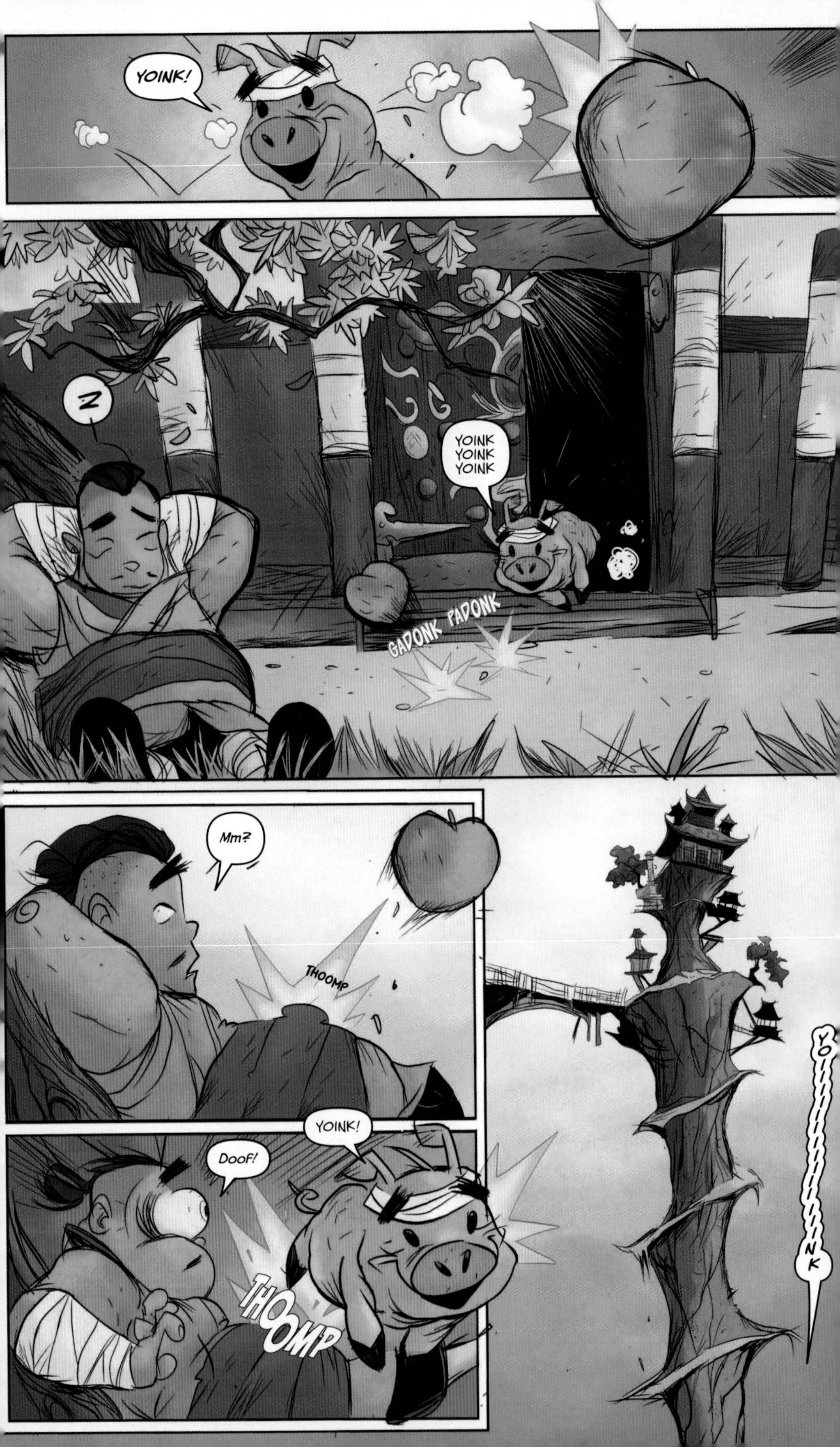
YOINK!
Z
YOINK YOINK YOINK
GADONK PADONK
Mm?
THOOMP
YOINK!
Doof!
THOOMP
YOIIIIIIIIIIINK

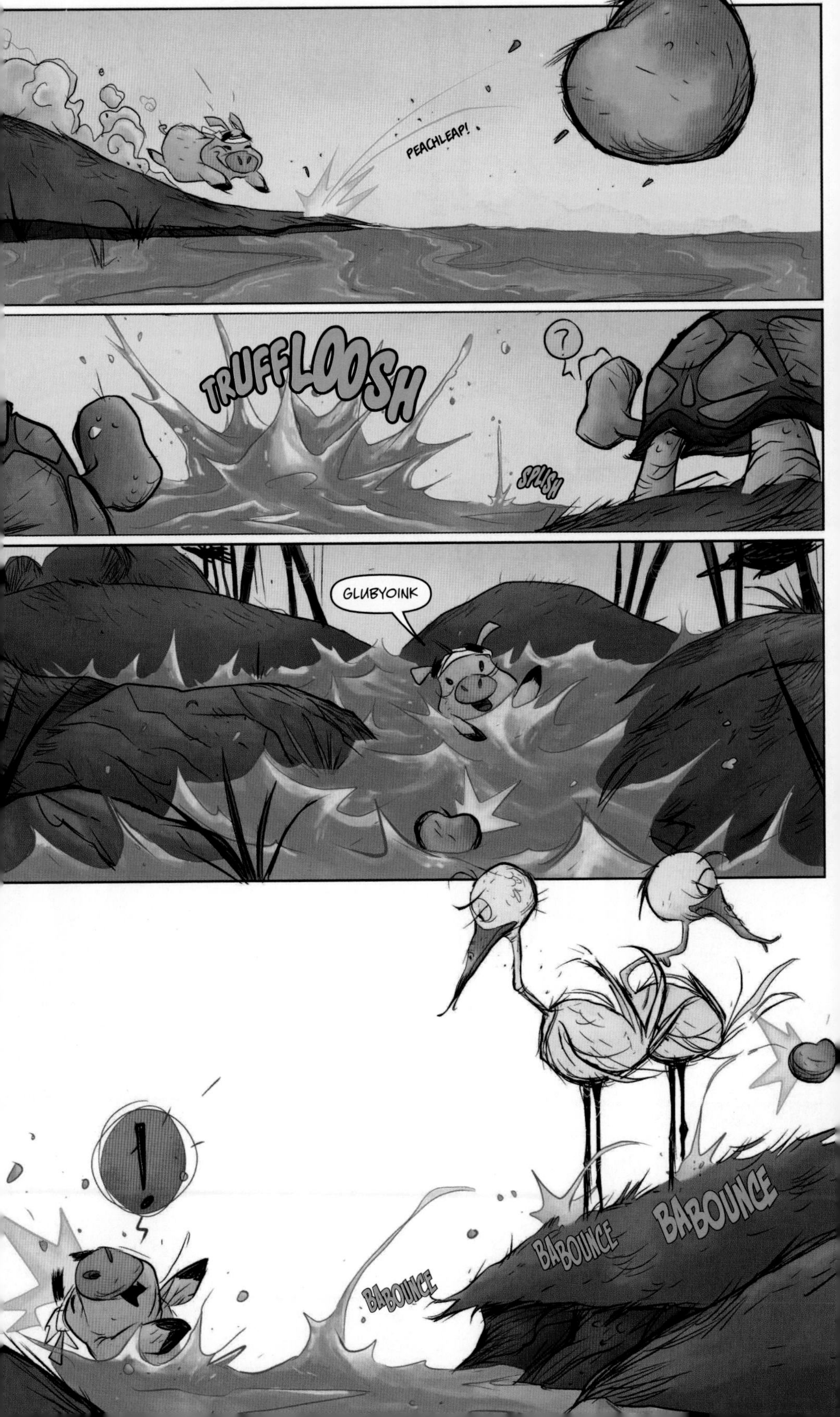

PEACHLEAP!
TRUFFLOOSH
?
SPLISH
GLUBYOINK
!
BABOUNCE
BABOUNCE
BABOUNCE

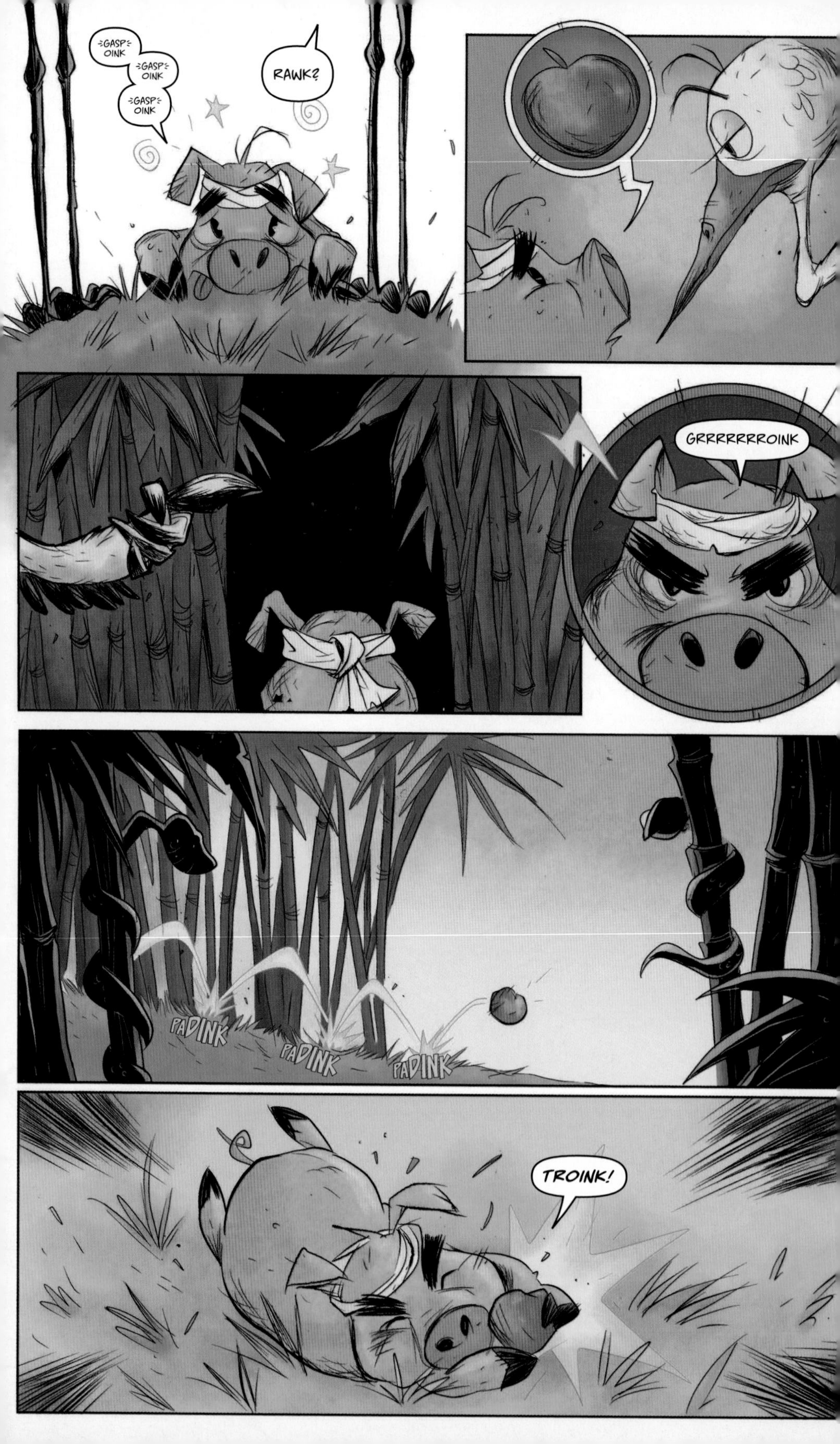

GASP OINK
GASP OINK
GASP OINK
RAWK?
GRRRRRRROINK
PADINK
PADINK
PADINK
TROINK!

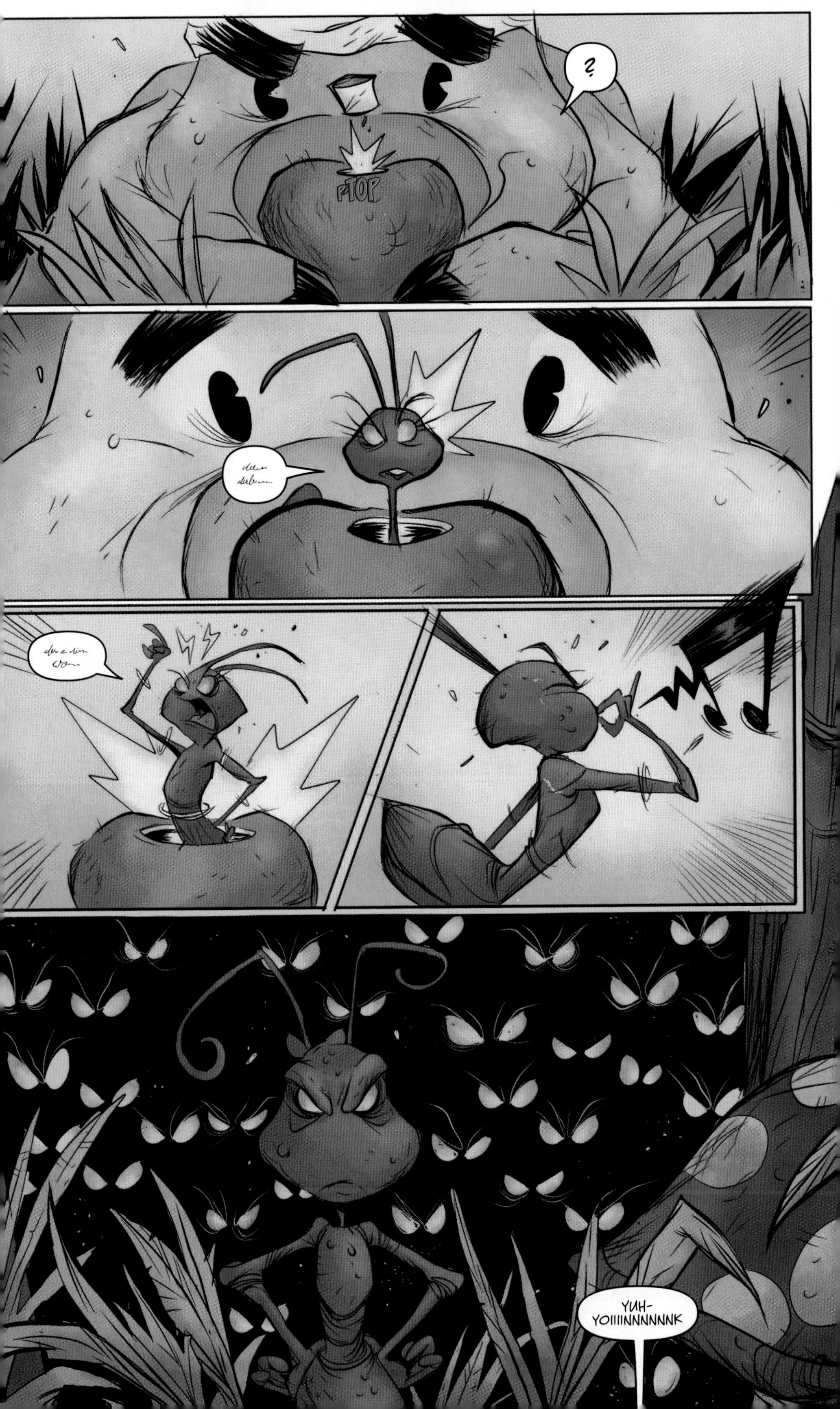
?
PTOP
YUH-
YOIIIINNNNNNK

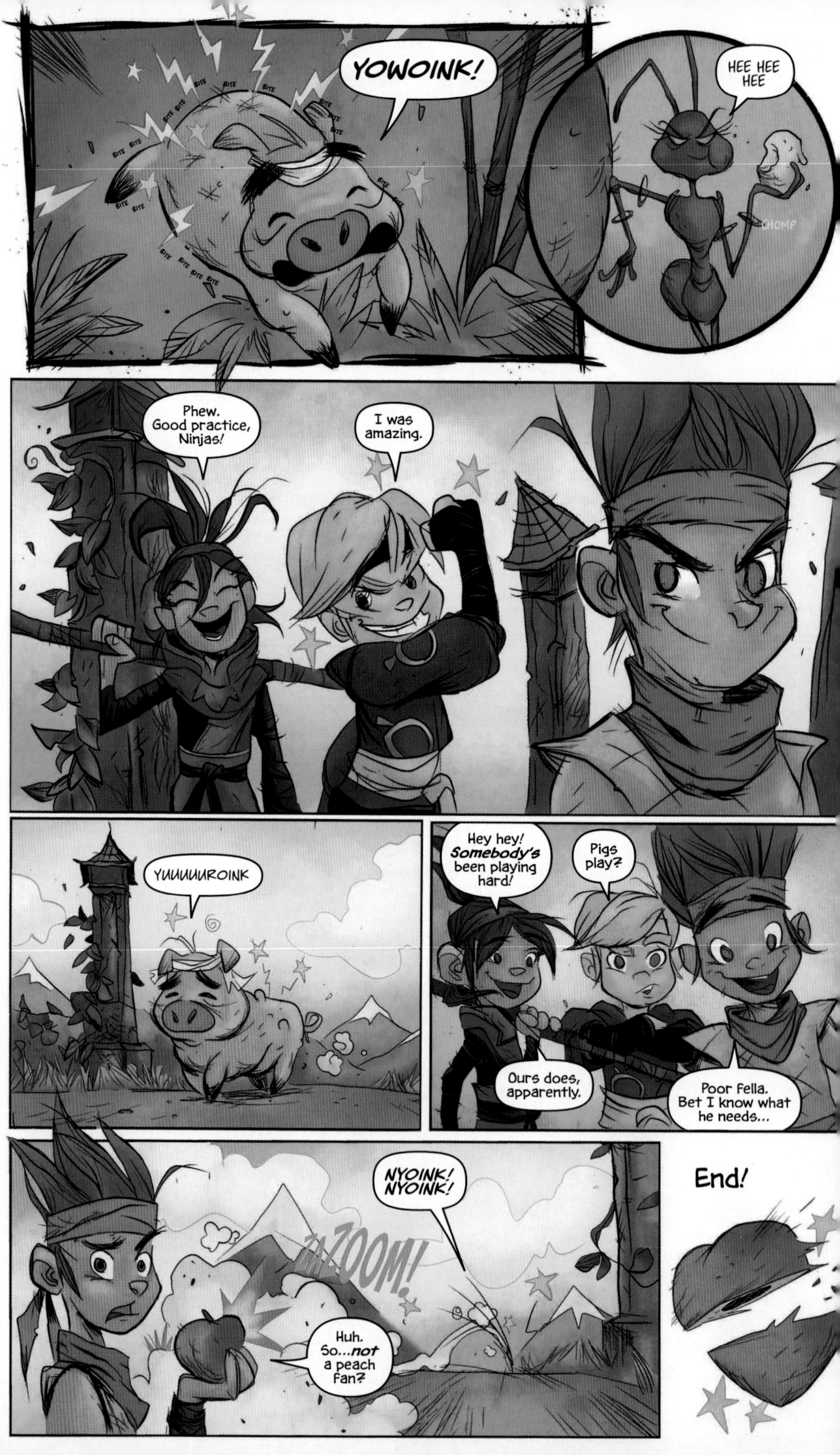
YOWOINK!
BITE BITE
HEE HEE HEE
CHOMP
Phew. Good practice, Ninjas!
I was amazing.
YUUUUUUROINK
Hey hey! Somebody's been playing hard!
Pigs play?
Ours does, apparently.
Poor fella. Bet I know what he needs...
NYOINK! NYOINK!
ZAZOOM!
Huh. So...not a peach fan?
End!

ND NOW...

THE THRILLING ORIGIN OF BARRY STEAKFRIES!

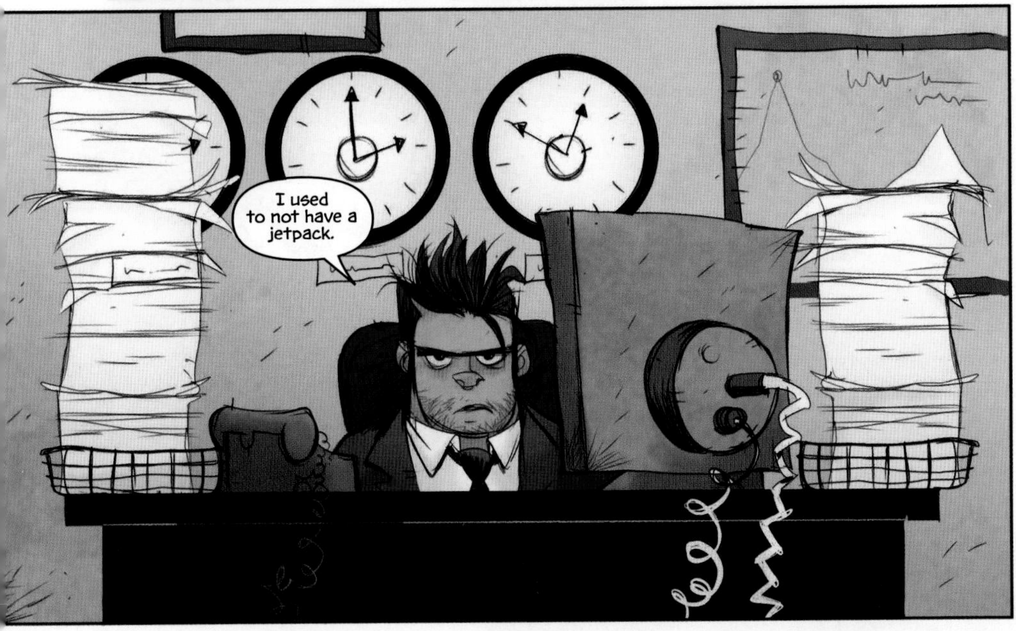

I used to not have a jetpack.

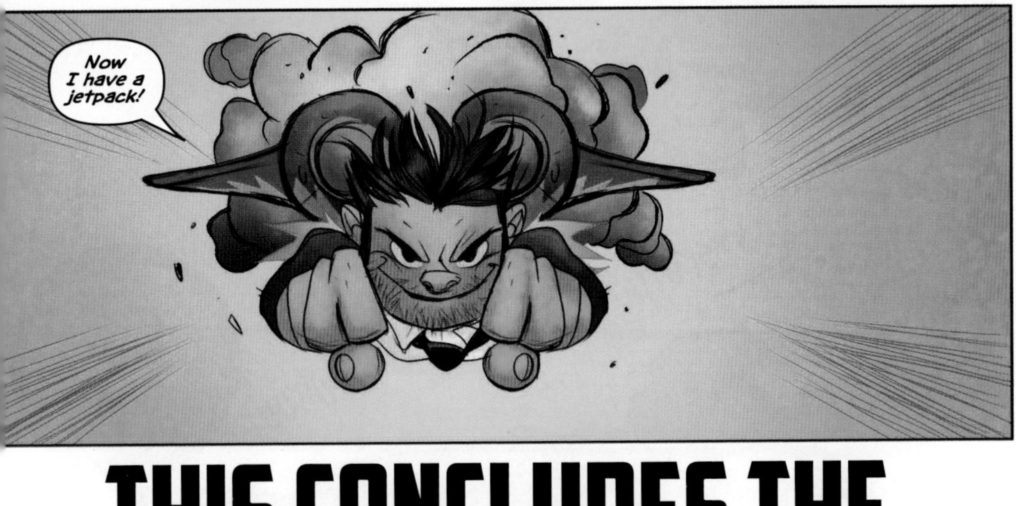

Now I have a jetpack!

THIS CONCLUDES THE THRILLING ORIGIN OF BARRY STEAKFRIES!

TODAY'S FEATURE...
"7 PAGES ABOUT HIPPOS & CAKE"

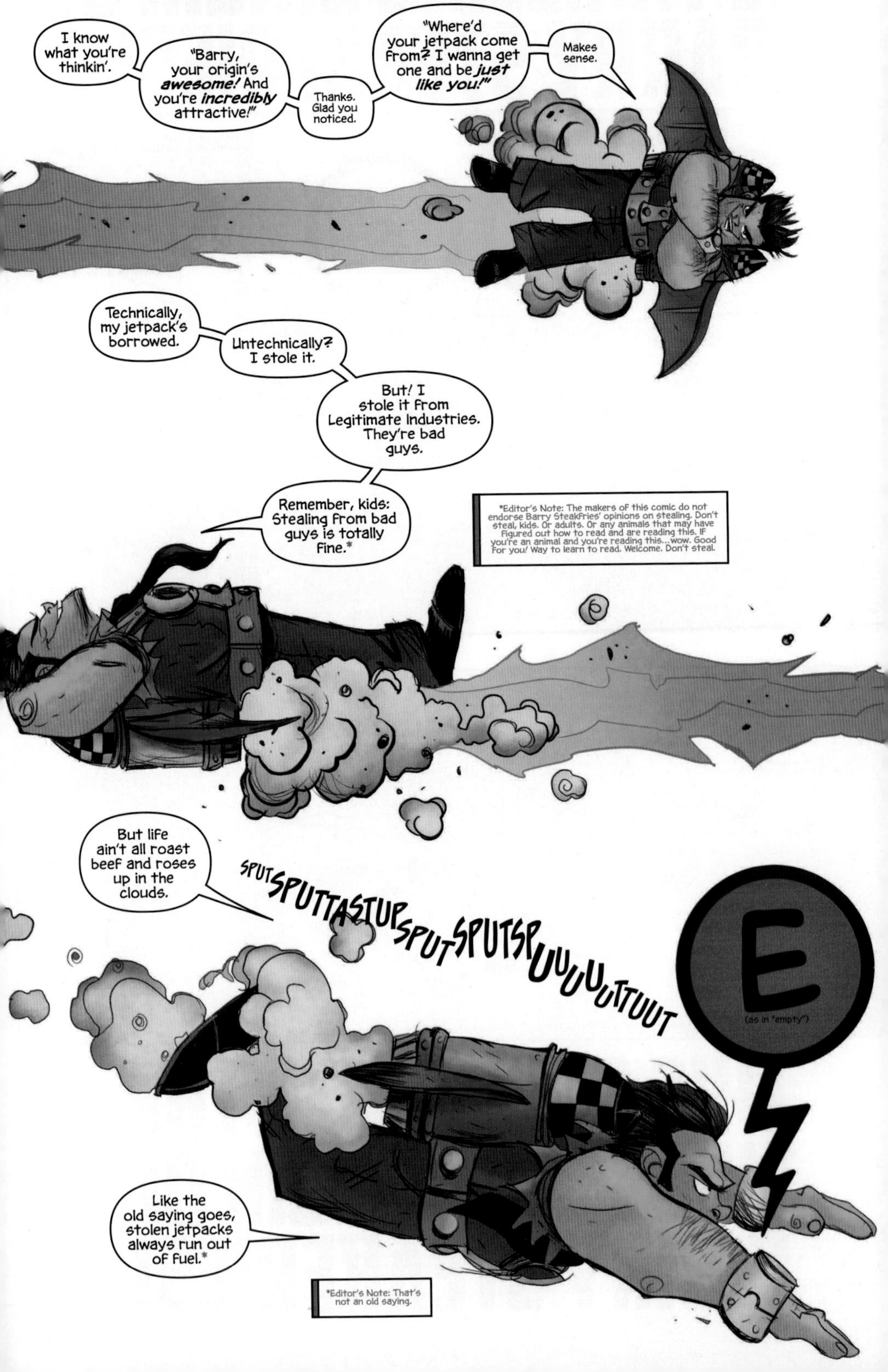

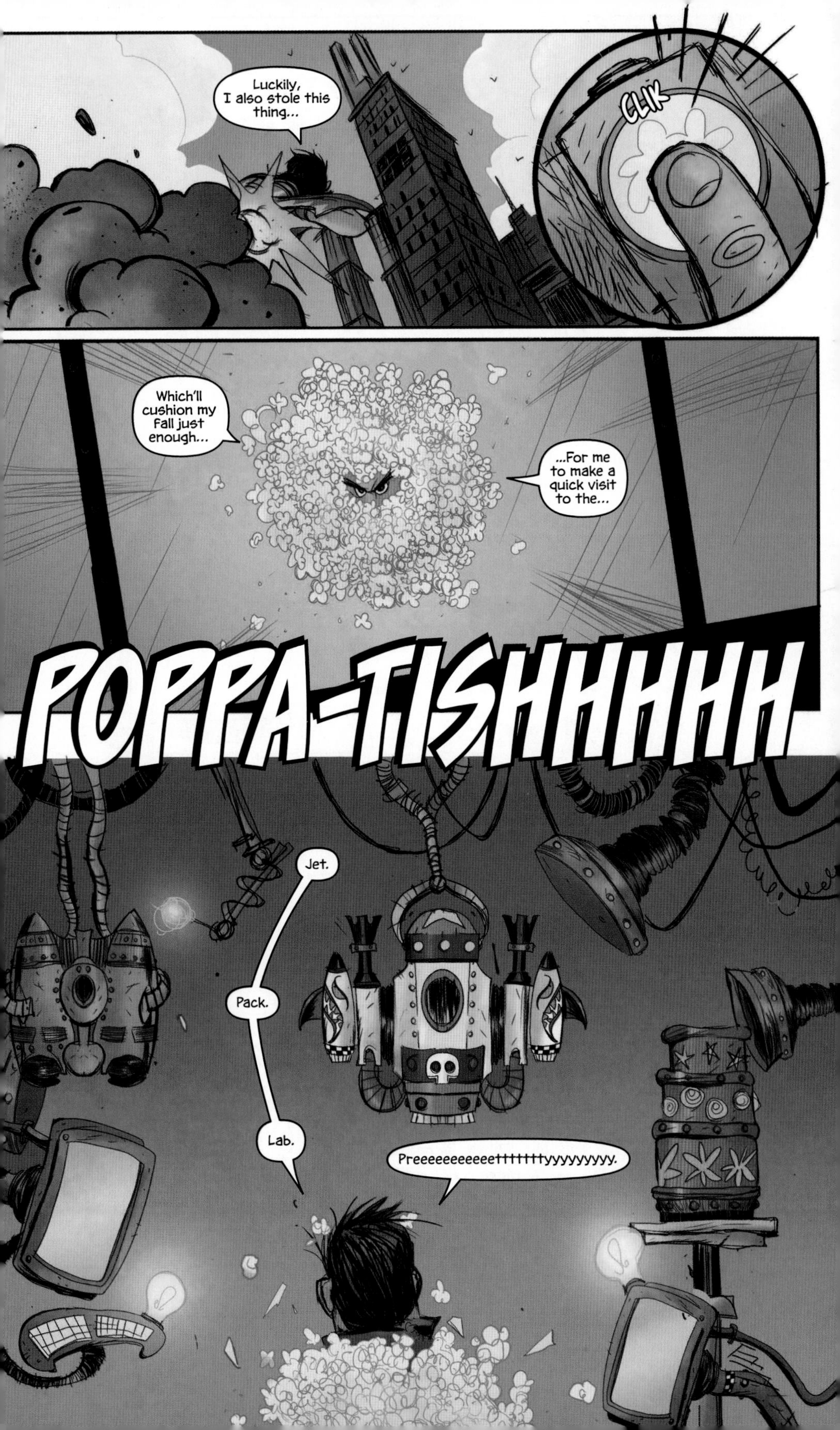

Luckily, I also stole this thing...
CLIK
Which'll cushion my fall just enough...
...For me to make a quick visit to the...
POPPA-TISHHHHHH
Jet.
Pack.
Lab.
Preeeeeeeeeeettttttttyyyyyyyyy.

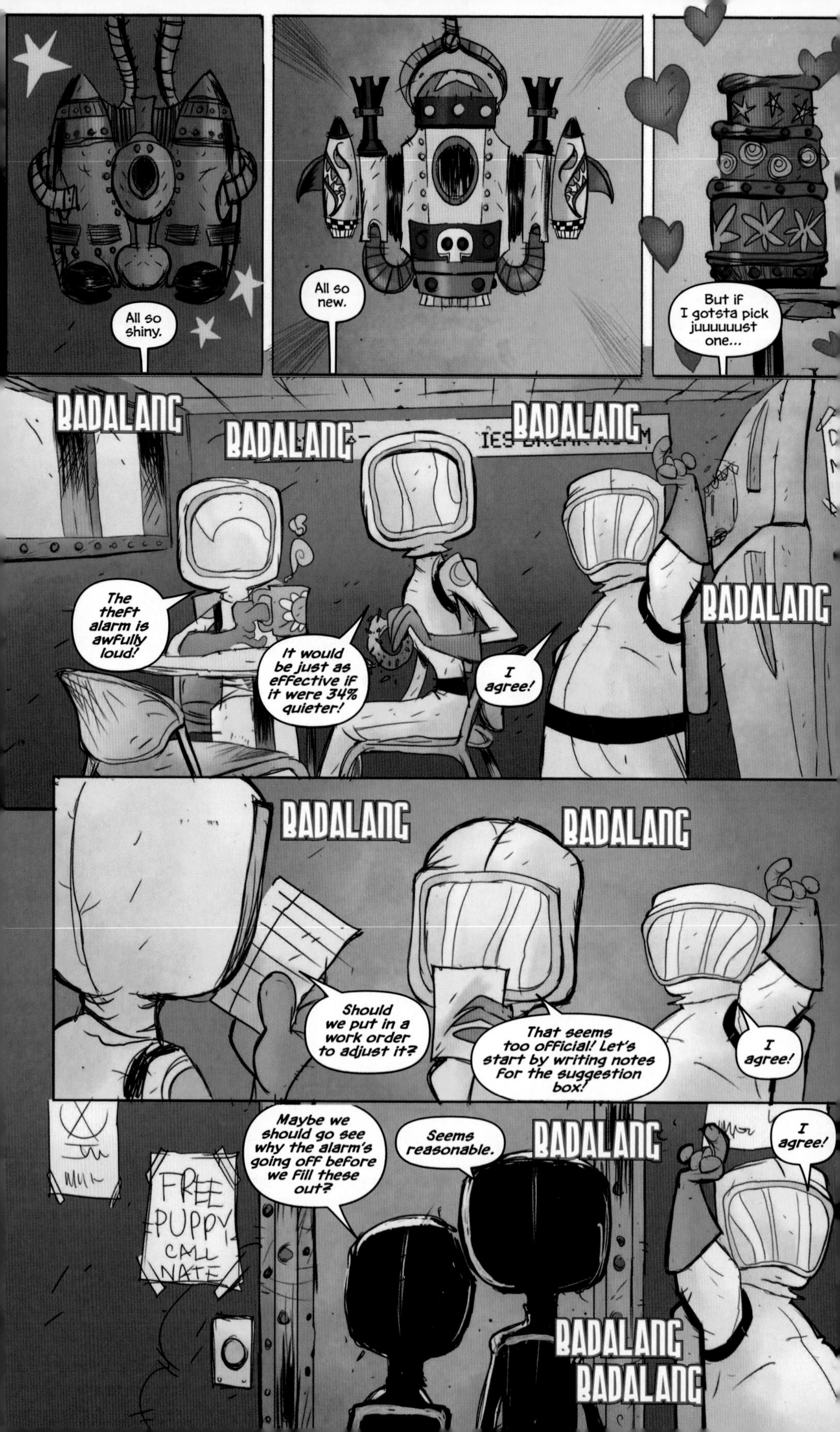
All so shiny.
All so new.
But if I gotsta pick juuuuuust one...
BADALANG
BADALANG
BADALANG
BADALANG
The theft alarm is awfully loud!
It would be just as effective if it were 34% quieter!
I agree!
BADALANG
BADALANG
Should we put in a work order to adjust it?
That seems too official! Let's start by writing notes for the suggestion box!
I agree!
Maybe we should go see why the alarm's going off before we fill these out?
Seems reasonable.
BADALANG
I agree!
FREE PUPPY CALL NATE
BADALANG
BADALANG

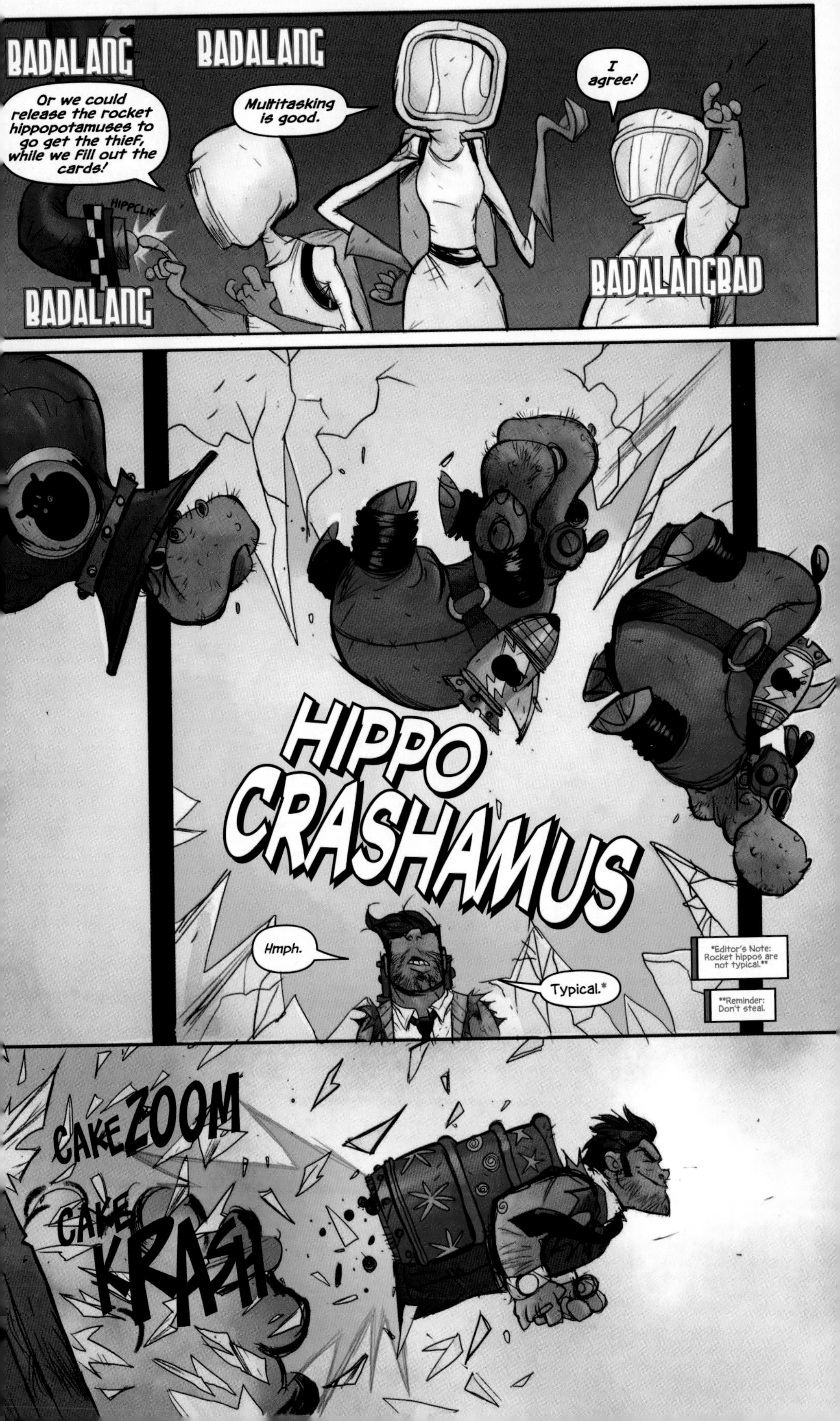

BADALANG
BADALANG
Or we could release the rocket hippopotamuses to go get the thief, while we fill out the cards!
Multitasking is good.
I agree!
HIPPCLIK
BADALANG
BADALANGBAD
HIPPO CRASHAMUS
Hmph.
Typical.*
*Editor's Note: Rocket hippos are not typical.**
**Reminder: Don't steal.
CAKEZOOM
CAKE KRASH

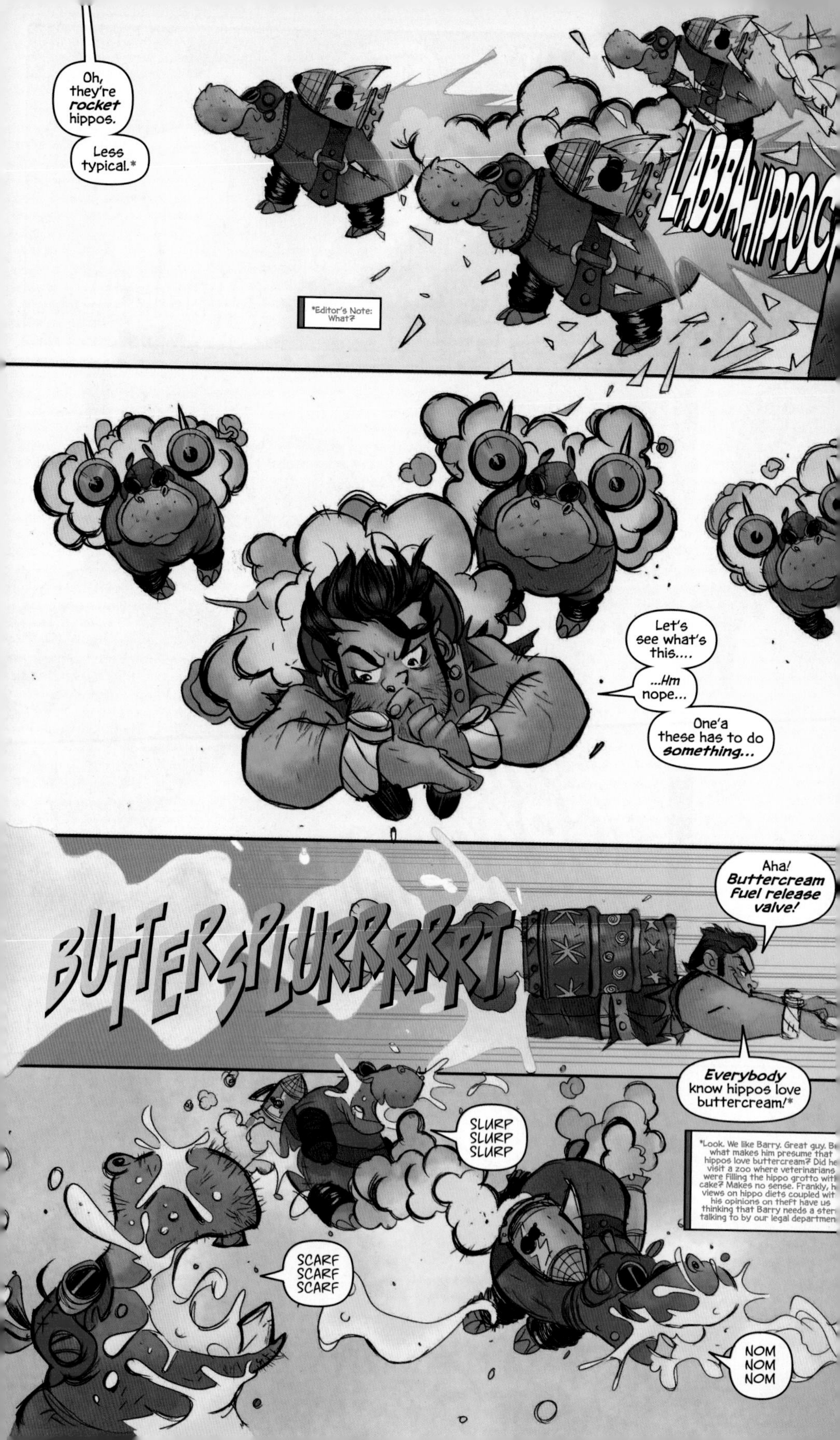

Oh, they're ***rocket*** hippos.
Less typical.*
LABBAHIPPOC
*Editor's Note: What?
Let's see what's this....
...Hm nope...
One'a these has to do ***something...***
BUTTERSPLURRRRRT
Aha! ***Buttercream fuel release valve!***
Everybody know hippos love buttercream!*
*Look. We like Barry. Great guy. B what makes him presume that hippos love buttercream? Did he visit a zoo where veterinarians were filling the hippo grotto wit cake? Makes no sense. Frankly, h views on hippo diets coupled wit his opinions on theft have us thinking that Barry needs a ster talking to by our legal departmen
SLURP SLURP SLURP
SCARF SCARF SCARF
NOM NOM NOM

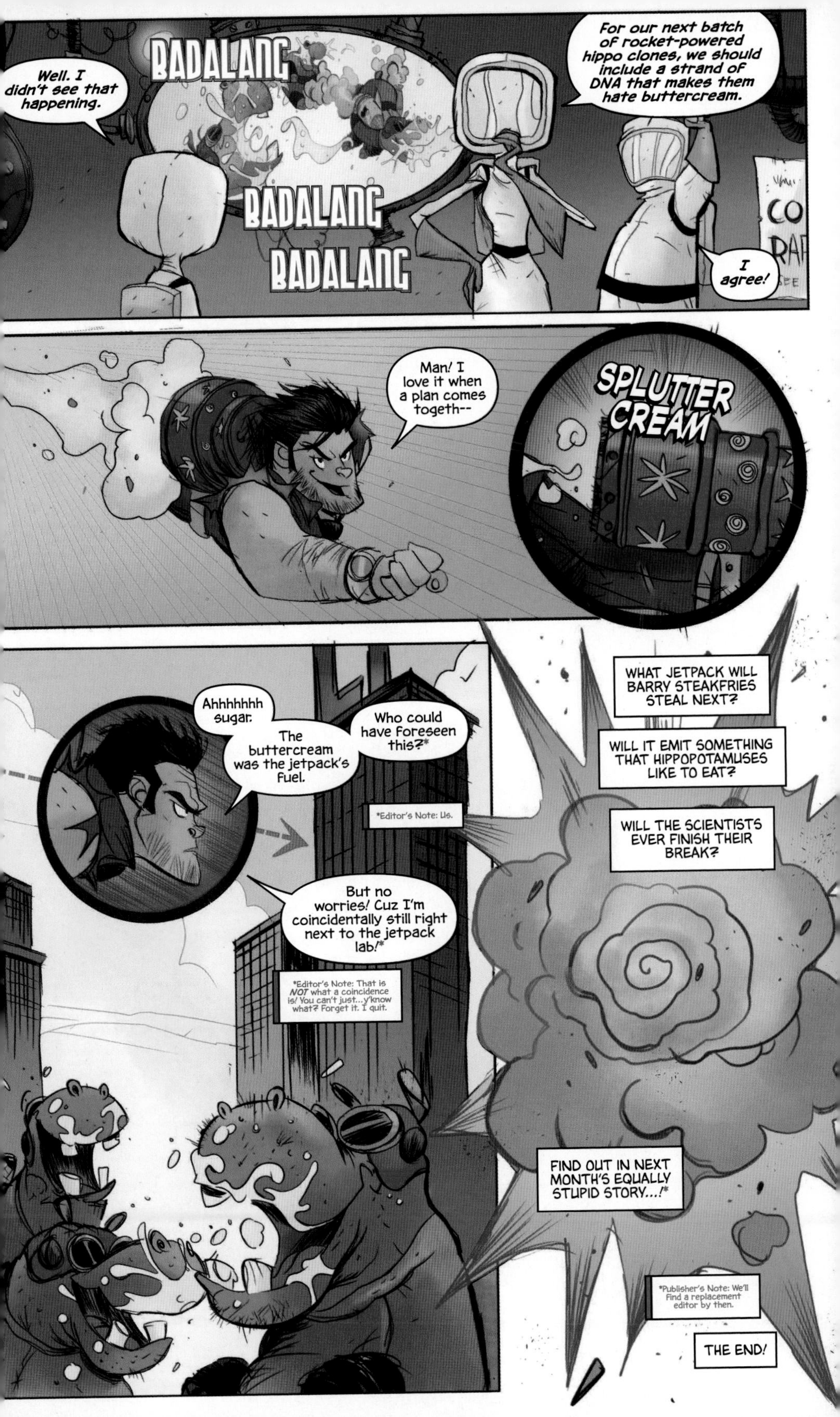

Well. I didn't see that happening.
BADALANG
BADALANG
BADALANG
For our next batch of rocket-powered hippo clones, we should include a strand of DNA that makes them hate buttercream.
I agree!
Man! I love it when a plan comes togeth--
SPLUTTER CREAM
Ahhhhhhh sugar.
The buttercream was the jetpack's fuel.
Who could have foreseen this?*
*Editor's Note: Us.
But no worries! Cuz I'm coincidentally still right next to the jetpack lab!*
*Editor's Note: That is NOT what a coincidence is! You can't just...y'know what? Forget it. I quit.
WHAT JETPACK WILL BARRY STEAKFRIES STEAL NEXT?
WILL IT EMIT SOMETHING THAT HIPPOPOTAMUSES LIKE TO EAT?
WILL THE SCIENTISTS EVER FINISH THEIR BREAK?
FIND OUT IN NEXT MONTH'S EQUALLY STUPID STORY...!*
*Publisher's Note: We'll find a replacement editor by then.
THE END!

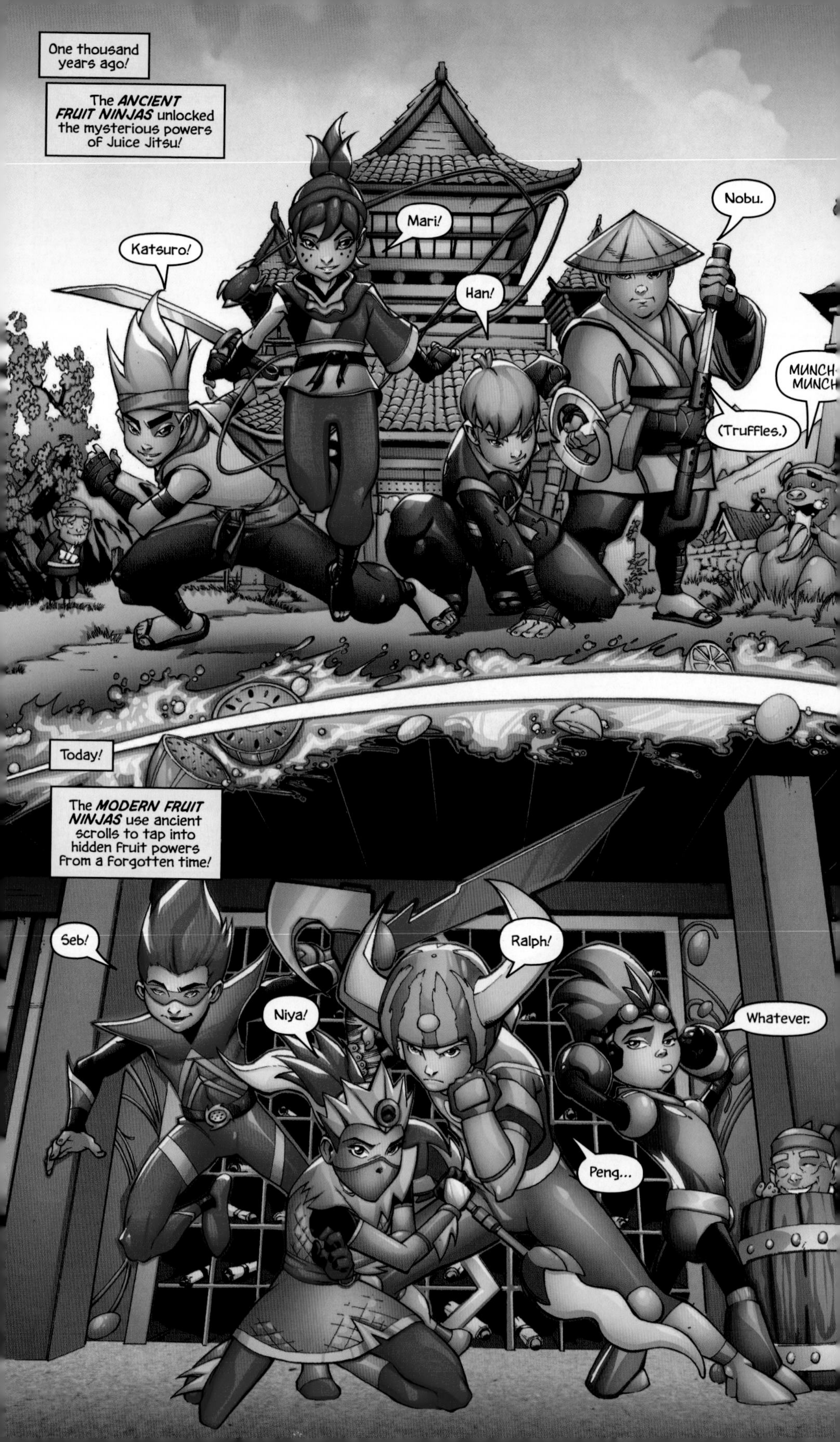
One thousand years ago!
The ANCIENT FRUIT NINJAS unlocked the mysterious powers of Juice Jitsu!
Katsuro!
Mari!
Han!
Nobu.
(Truffles.)
MUNCH-MUNCH
Today!
The MODERN FRUIT NINJAS use ancient scrolls to tap into hidden fruit powers from a forgotten time!
Seb!
Niya!
Ralph!
Whatever.
Peng...

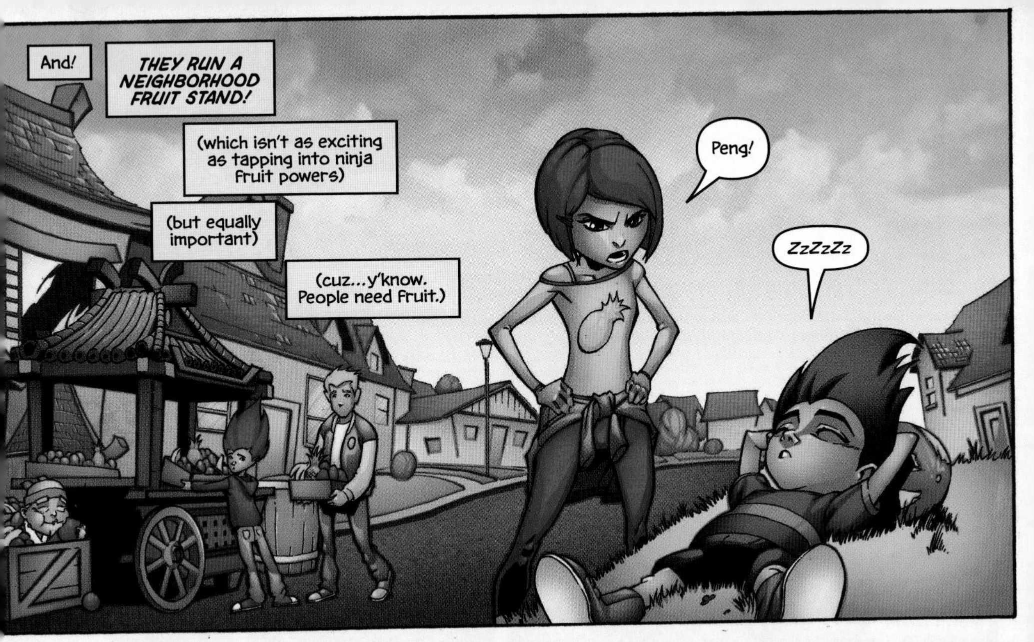
And!
THEY RUN A NEIGHBORHOOD FRUIT STAND!
(which isn't as exciting as tapping into ninja fruit powers)
(but equally important)
(cuz...y'know. People need fruit.)
Peng!
ZzZzZz

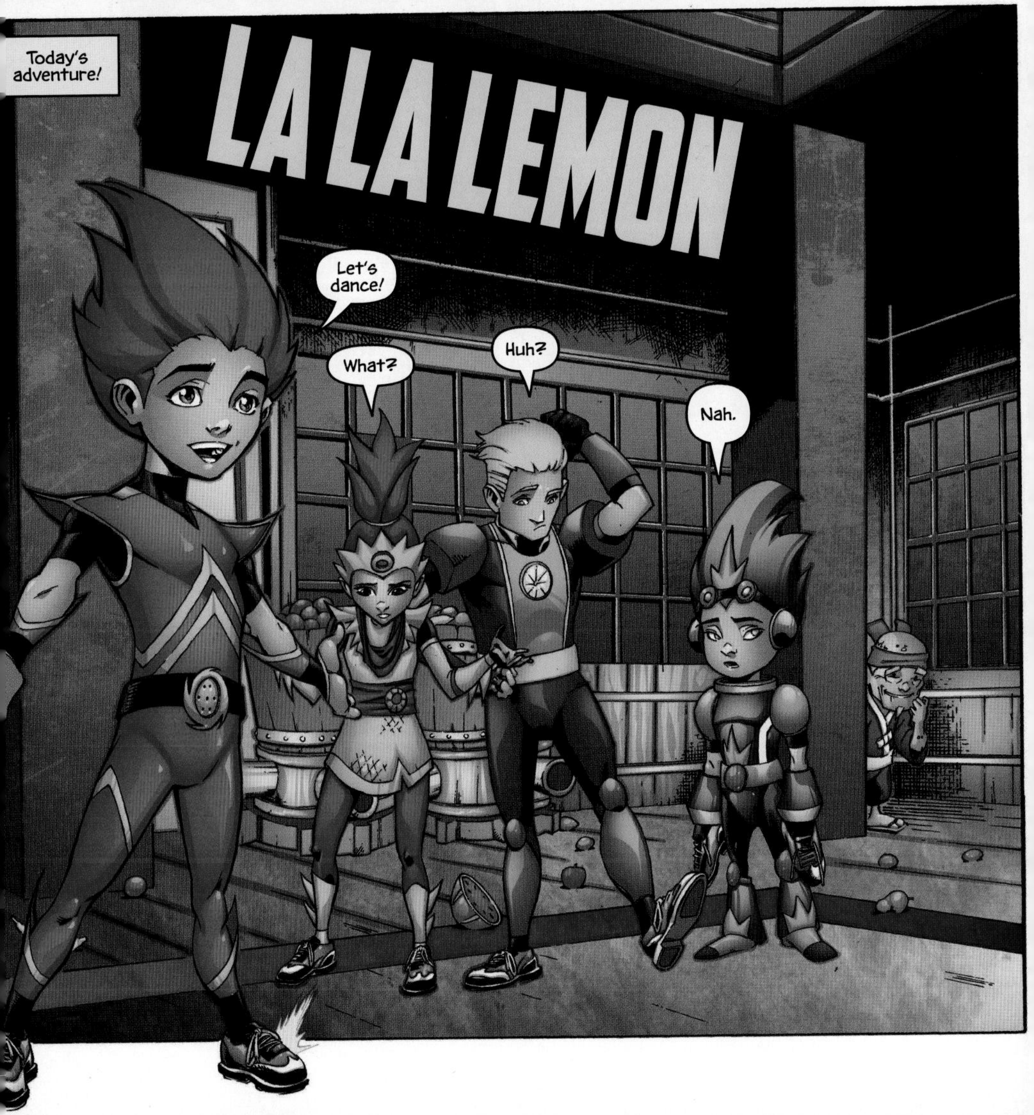
Today's adventure!
LA LA LEMON
Let's dance!
What?
Huh?
Nah.

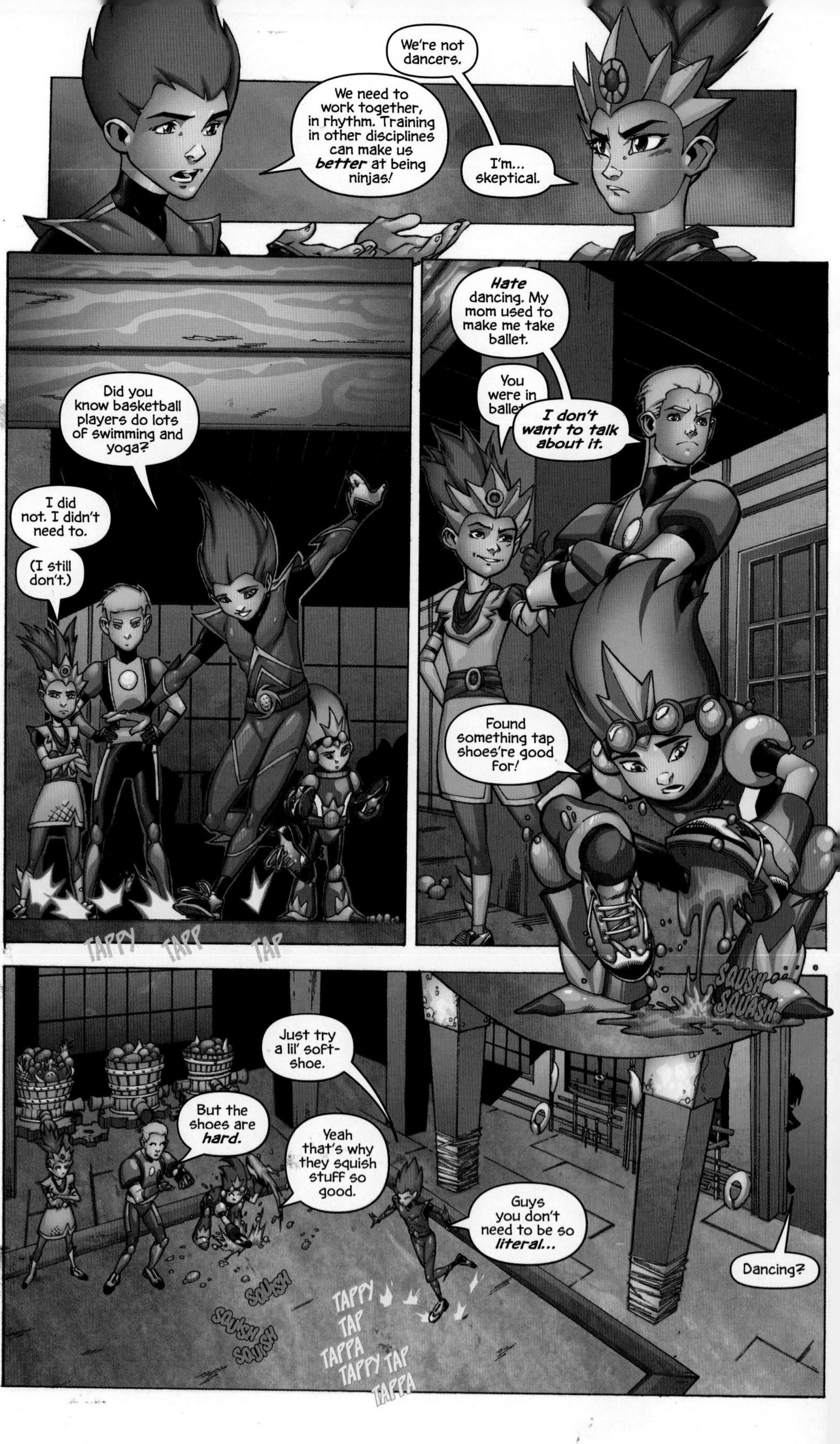
We need to work together, in rhythm. Training in other disciplines can make us *better* at being ninjas!
We're not dancers.
I'm... skeptical.
Did you know basketball players do lots of swimming and yoga?
I did not. I didn't need to.
(I still don't.)
TAPPY
TAPP
TAP
Hate dancing. My mom used to make me take ballet.
You were in ballet
I don't want to talk about it.
Found something tap shoes're good for!
SQUISH
SQUASH
Just try a lil' soft-shoe.
But the shoes are *hard.*
Yeah that's why they squish stuff so good.
Guys you don't need to be so *literal...*
Dancing?
SQUISH
SQUISH
SQUISH
TAPPY
TAP
TAPPA
TAPPY TAP
TAPPA

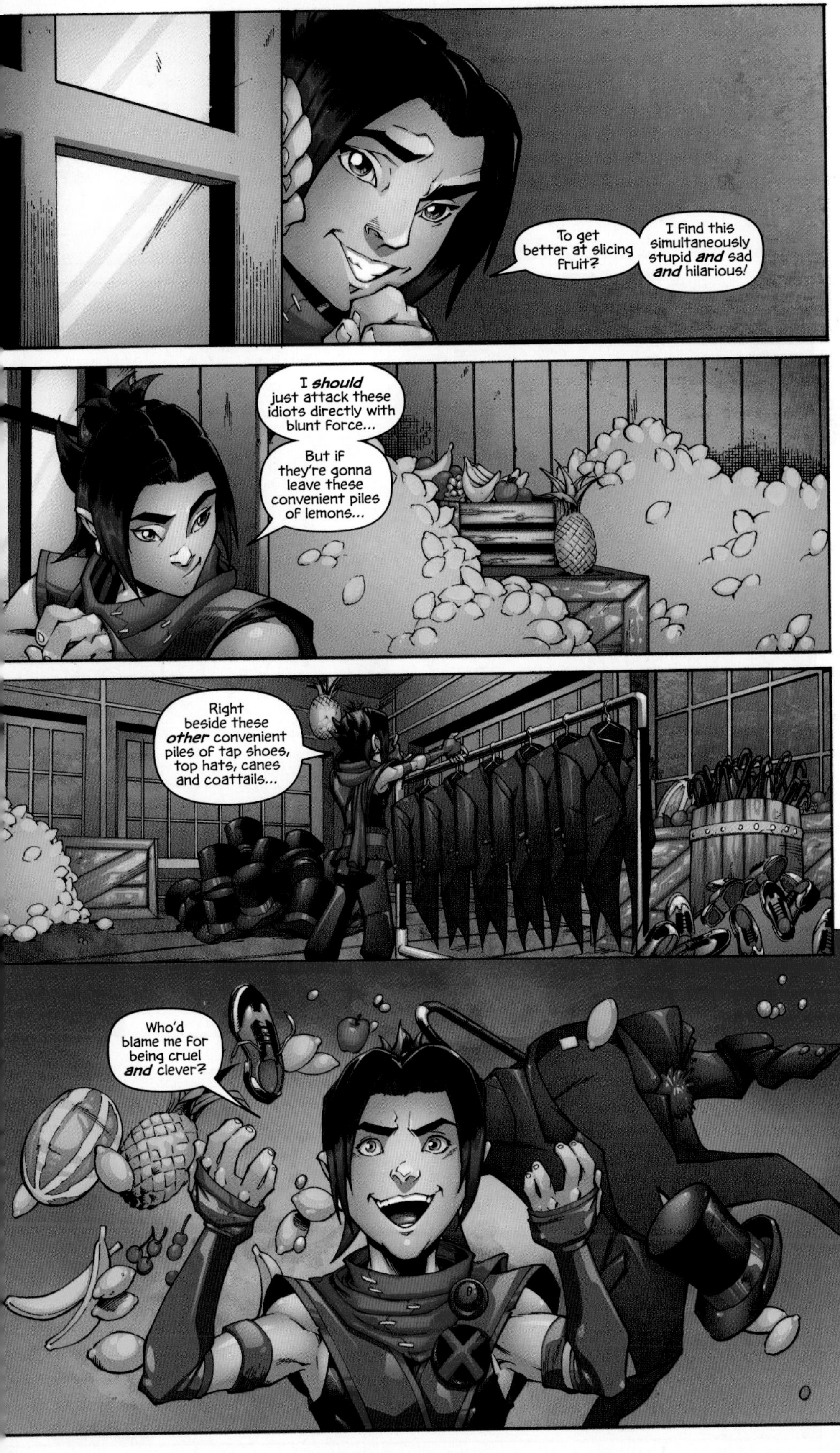
To get better at slicing fruit?
I find this simultaneously stupid *and* sad *and* hilarious!
I *should* just attack these idiots directly with blunt force...
But if they're gonna leave these convenient piles of lemons...
Right beside these *other* convenient piles of tap shoes, top hats, canes and coattails...
Who'd blame me for being cruel *and* clever?

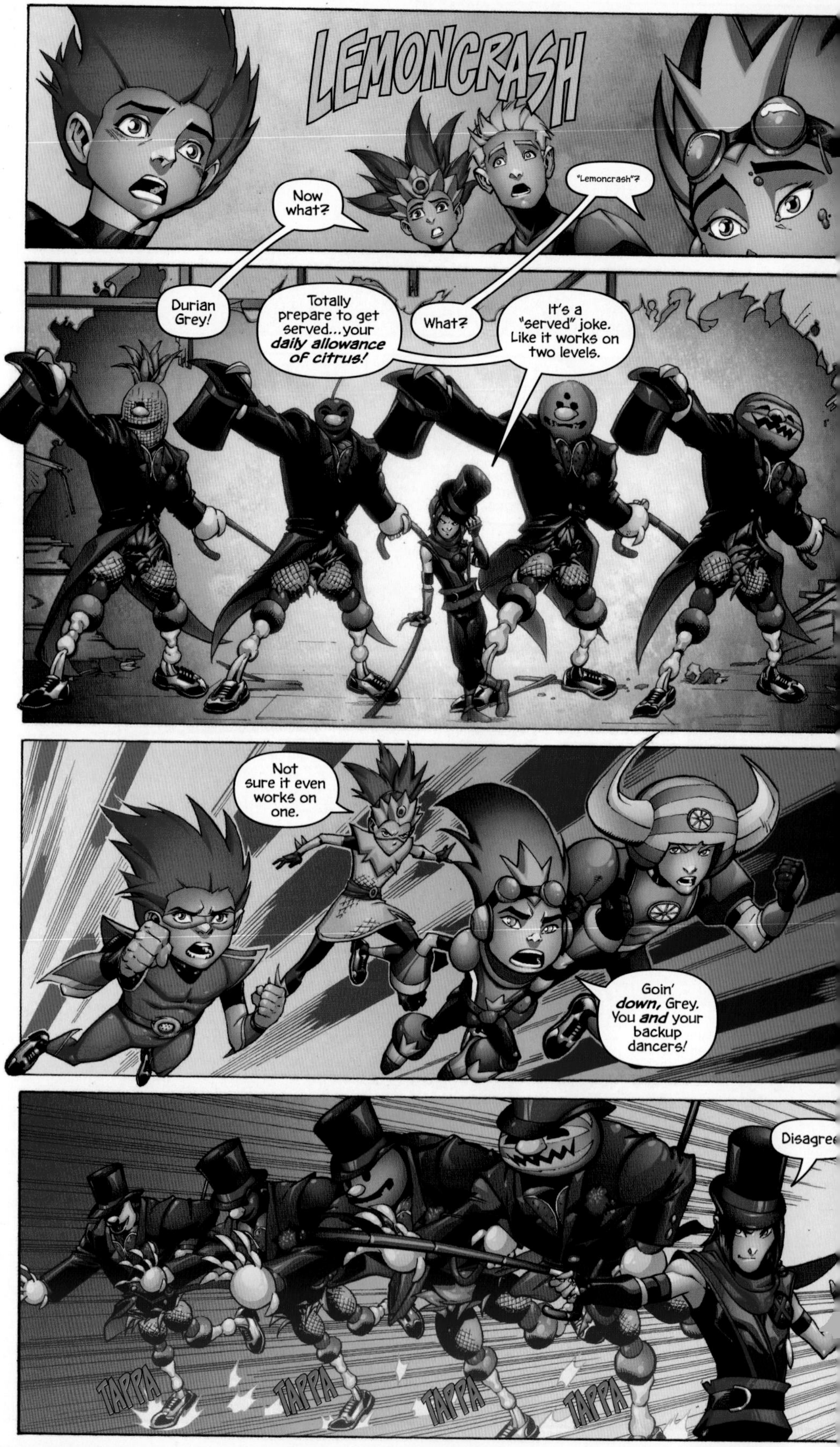
LEMONCRASH
Now what?
"Lemoncrash"?
Durian Grey!
Totally prepare to get served...your *daily allowance of citrus!*
What?
It's a "served" joke. Like it works on two levels.
Not sure it even works on one.
Goin' ***down,*** Grey. You ***and*** your backup dancers!
Disagre
TAPPA
TAPPA
TAPPA
TAPPA

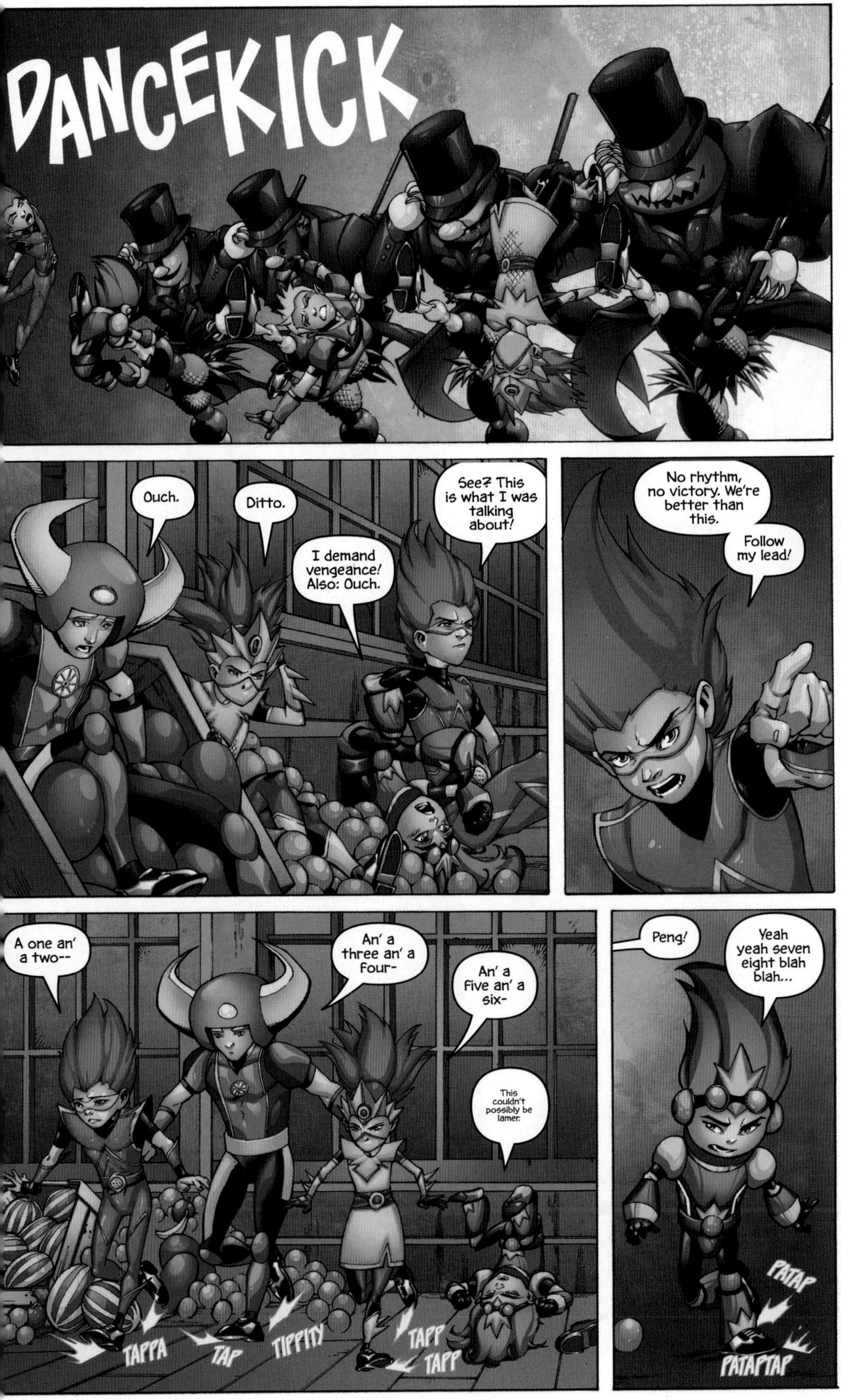
DANCEKICK
Ouch.
Ditto.
I demand vengeance! Also: Ouch.
See? This is what I was talking about!
No rhythm, no victory. We're better than this.
Follow my lead!
A one an' a two--
An' a three an' a four-
An' a five an' a six-
This couldn't possibly be lamer.
TAPPA
TAP
TIPPITY
TAPP
TAPP
Peng!
Yeah yeah seven eight blah blah...
PATAP
PATAPTAP

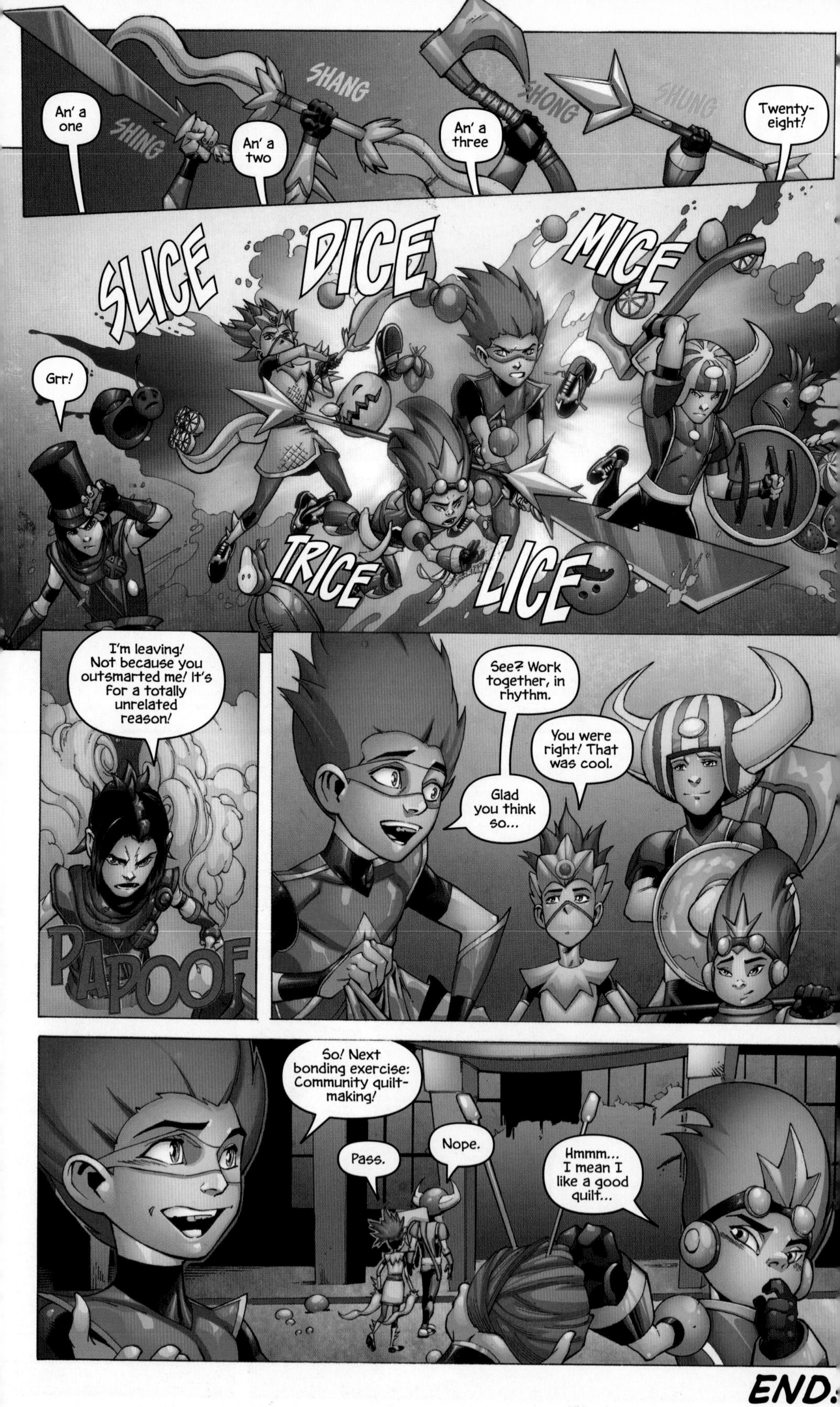
An' a one
SHING
An' a two
SHANG
An' a three
SHONG
SHUNG
Twenty-eight!
SLICE
DICE
MICE
Grr!
TRICE
LICE
I'm leaving! Not because you outsmarted me! It's for a totally unrelated reason!
PAPOOF
See? Work together, in rhythm.
You were right! That was cool.
Glad you think so...
So! Next bonding exercise: Community quilt-making!
Pass.
Nope.
Hmmm... I mean I like a good quilt...

END.

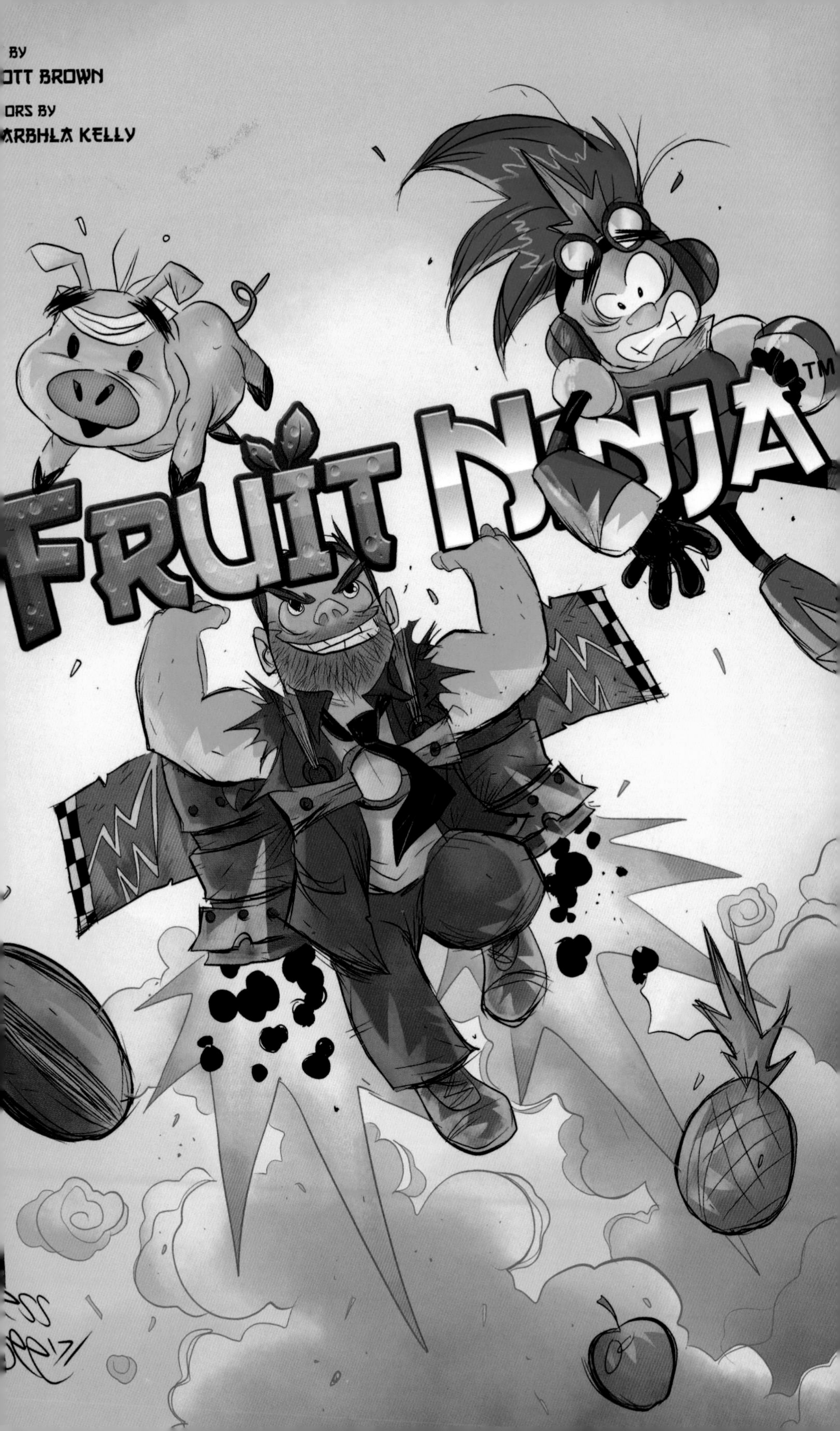
BY
OTT BROWN
ORS BY
ARBHLA KELLY
FRUIT NINJA™

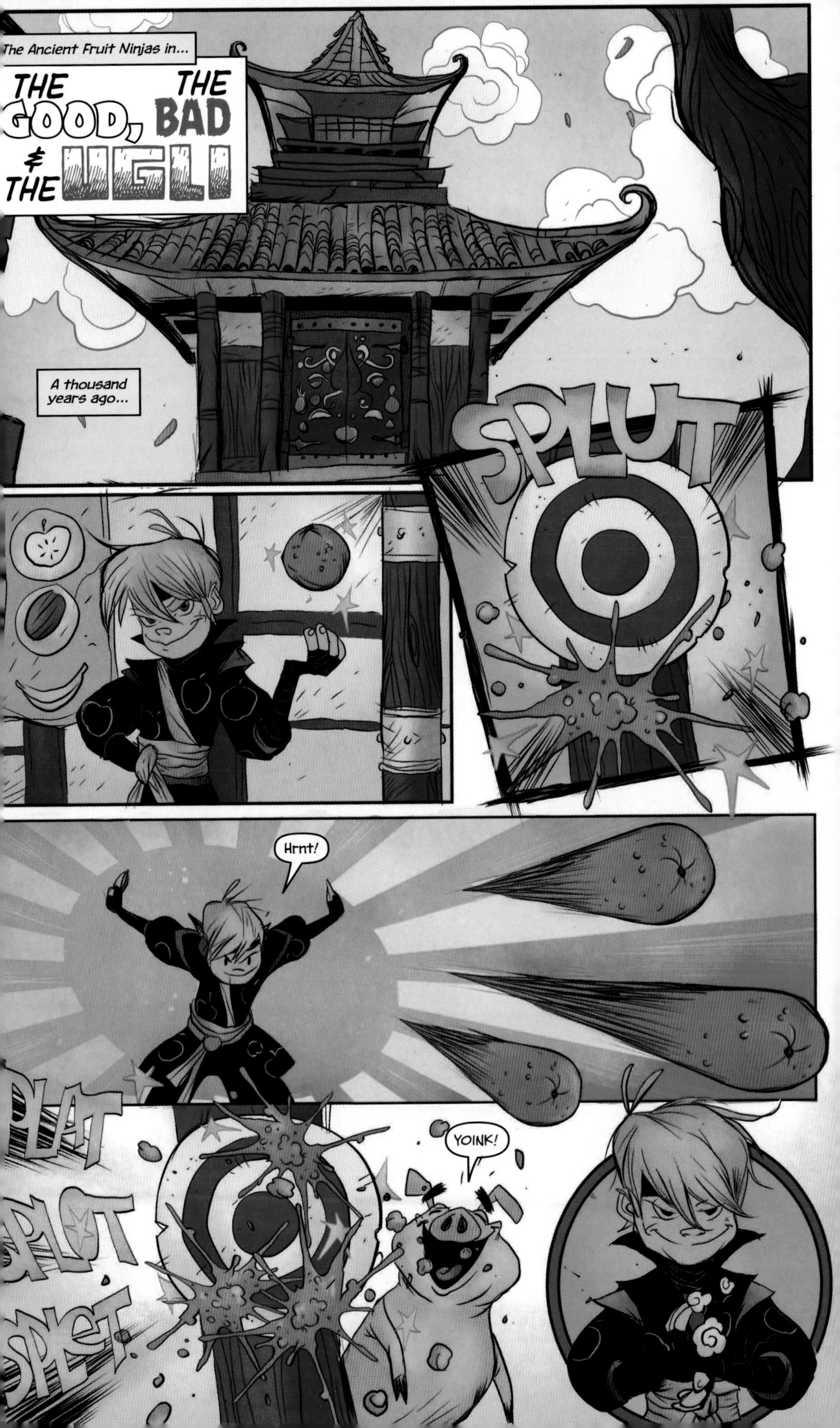
The Ancient Fruit Ninjas in...
THE GOOD, THE BAD & THE UGLI
A thousand years ago...
SPLUT
Hrnt!
SPLAT
SPLUT
SPLET
YOINK!

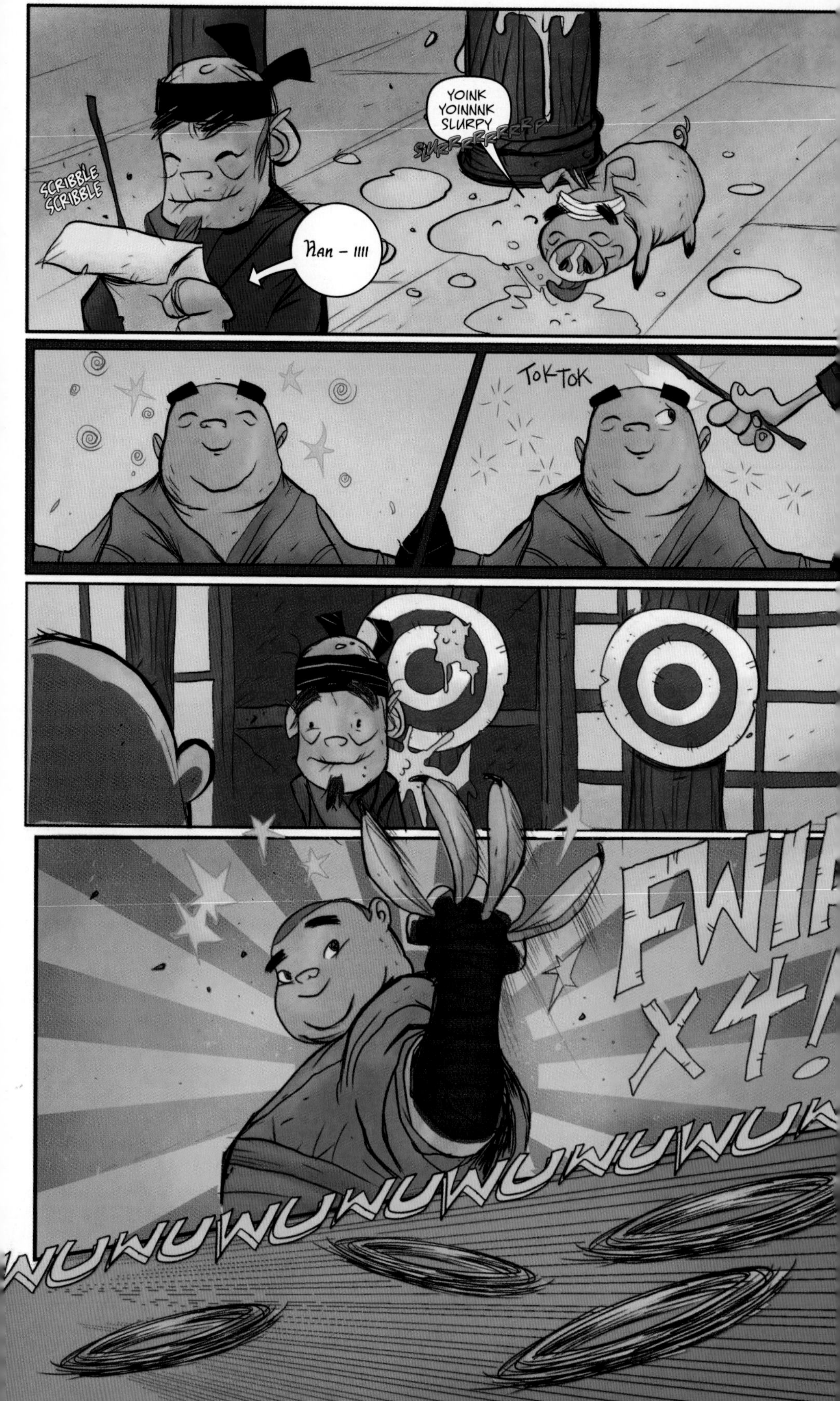

SCRIBBLE SCRIBBLE
YOINK YOINNNK SLURPY
SLURRRRRRRRP
Nan - IIII
TOK TOK
FWIP X4!
WUWUWUWUWUWUWUWUWUWUK

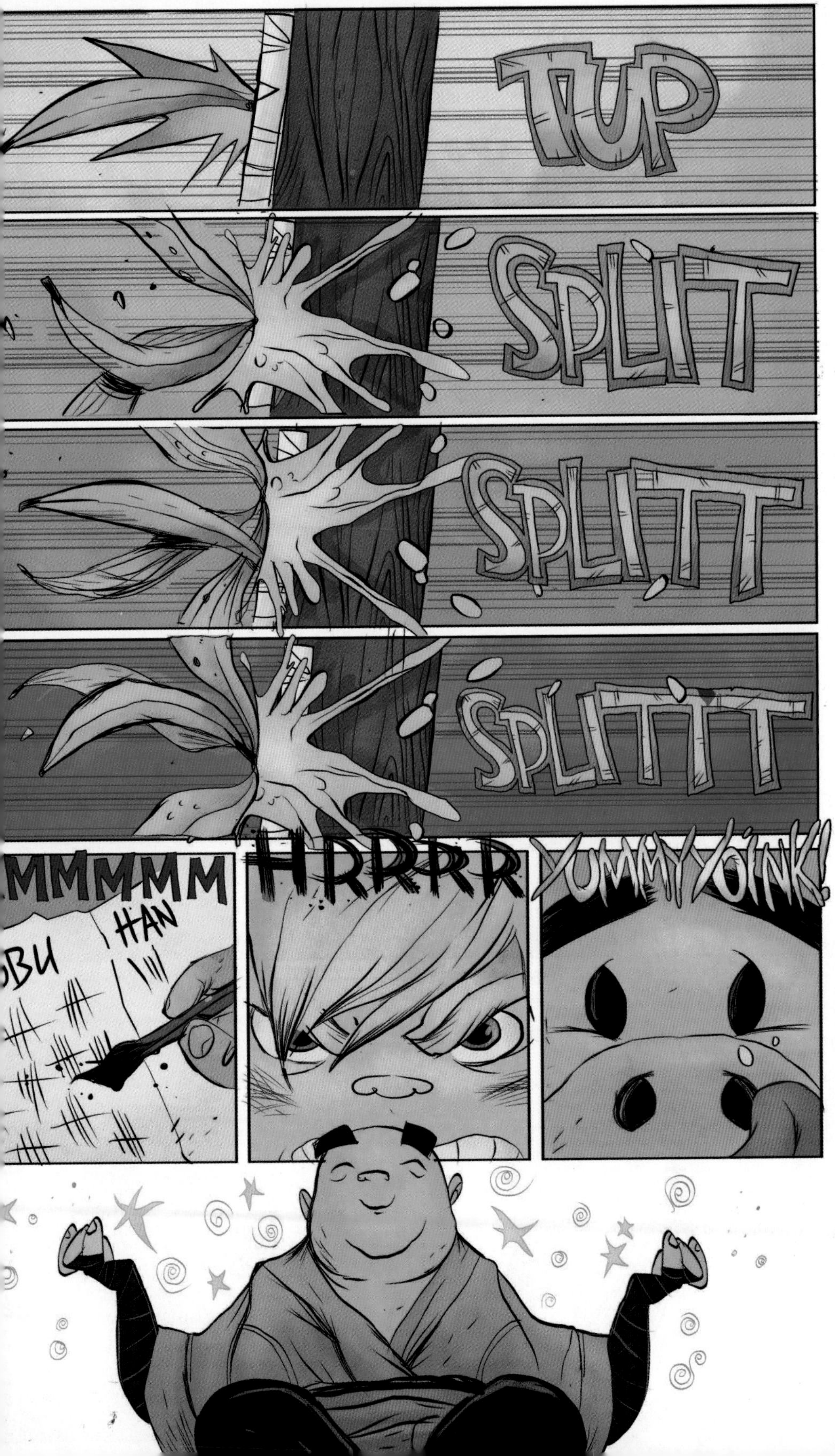
TUP
SPLIT
SPLITT
SPLITTT
MMMMMM
BU
HAN
HRRRRR
YUMMYYOINK!

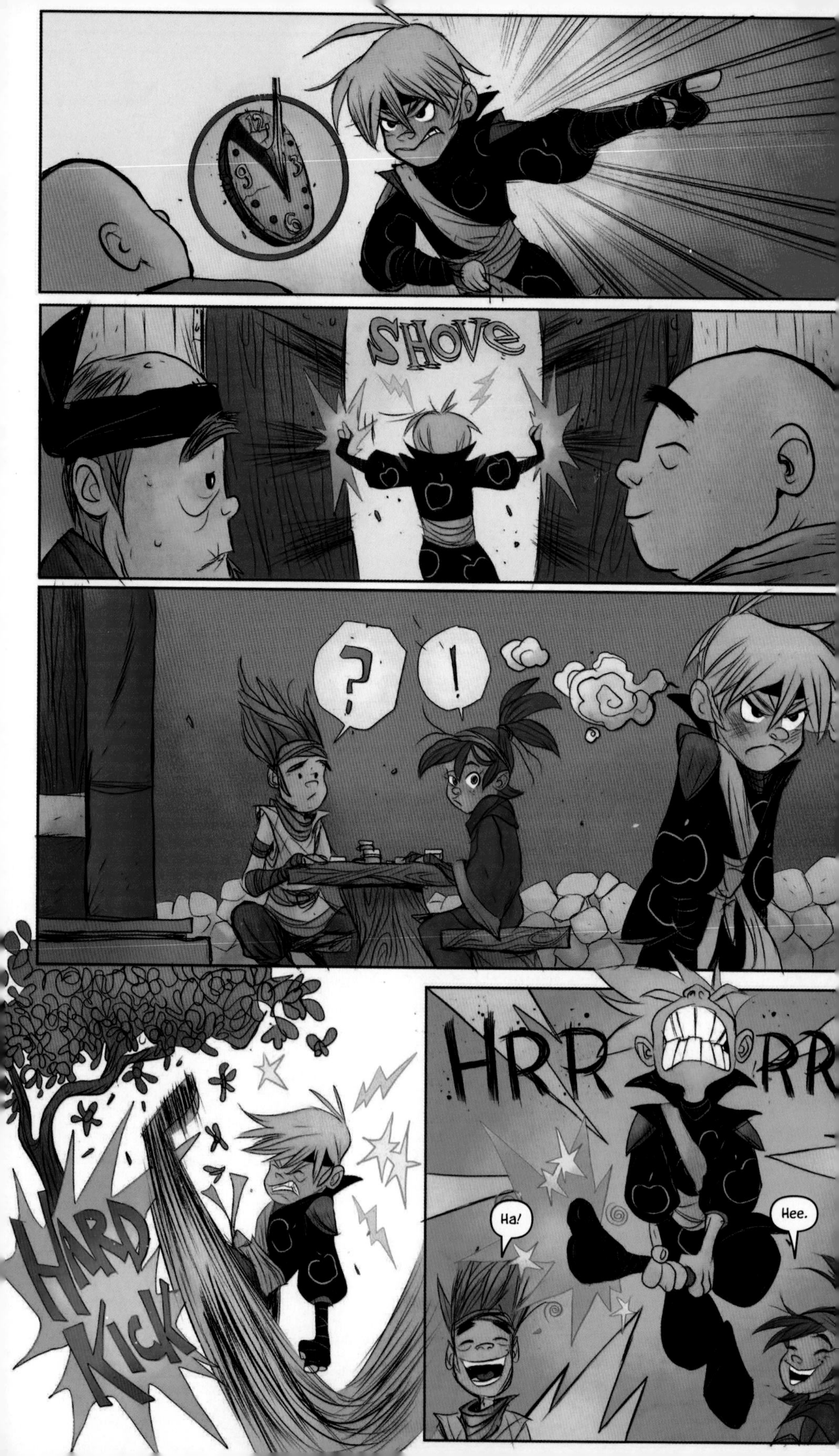
SHOVE
?
!
HARD KICK
HRR RR
Ha!
Hee.

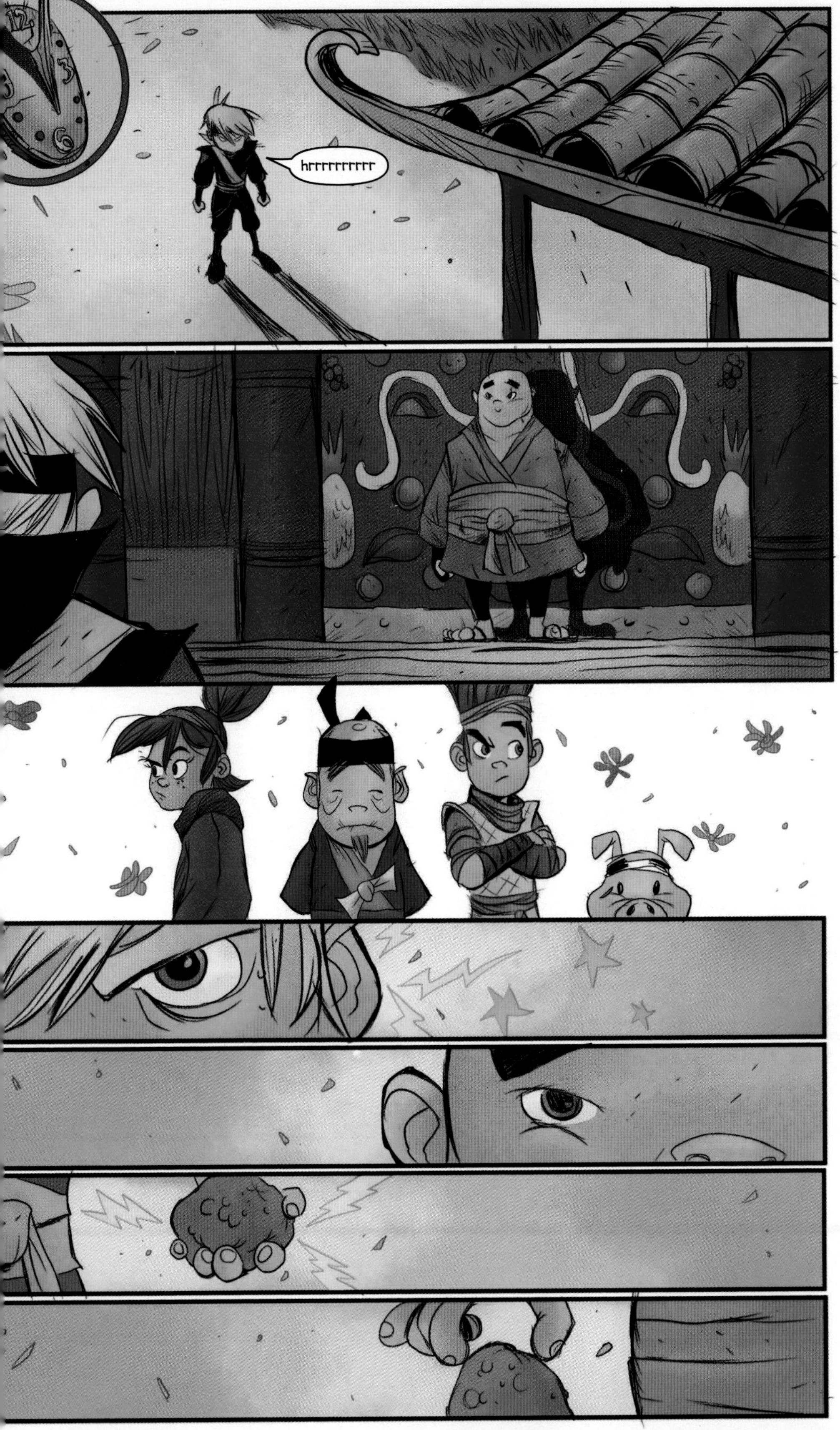
hrrrrrrrrrr

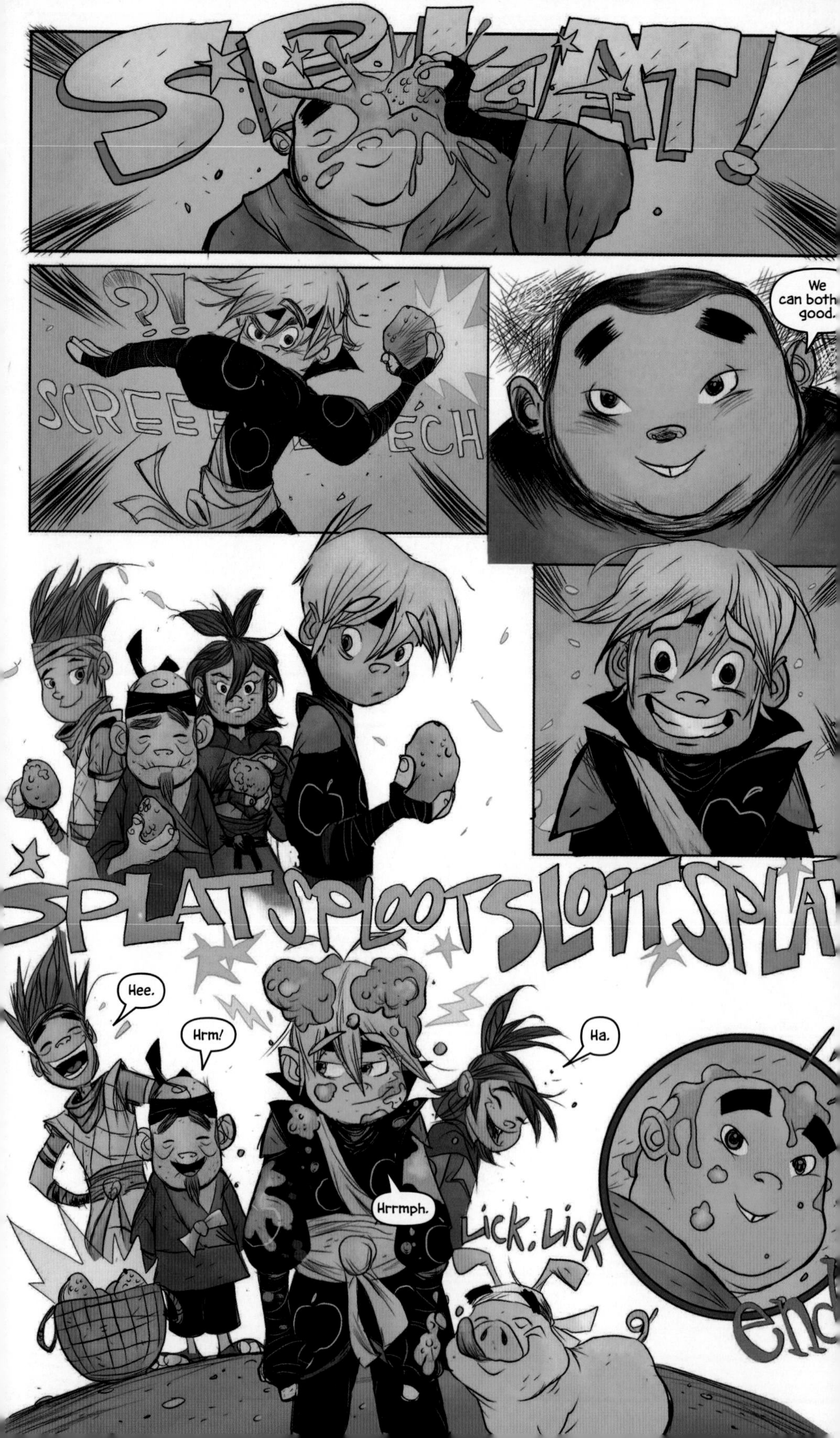
SPLAT!
?!
SCREEECH
We can both good.
SPLAT SPLOOT SLOIT SPLA
Hee.
Hrm!
Ha.
Hrrmph.
Lick. Lick
end

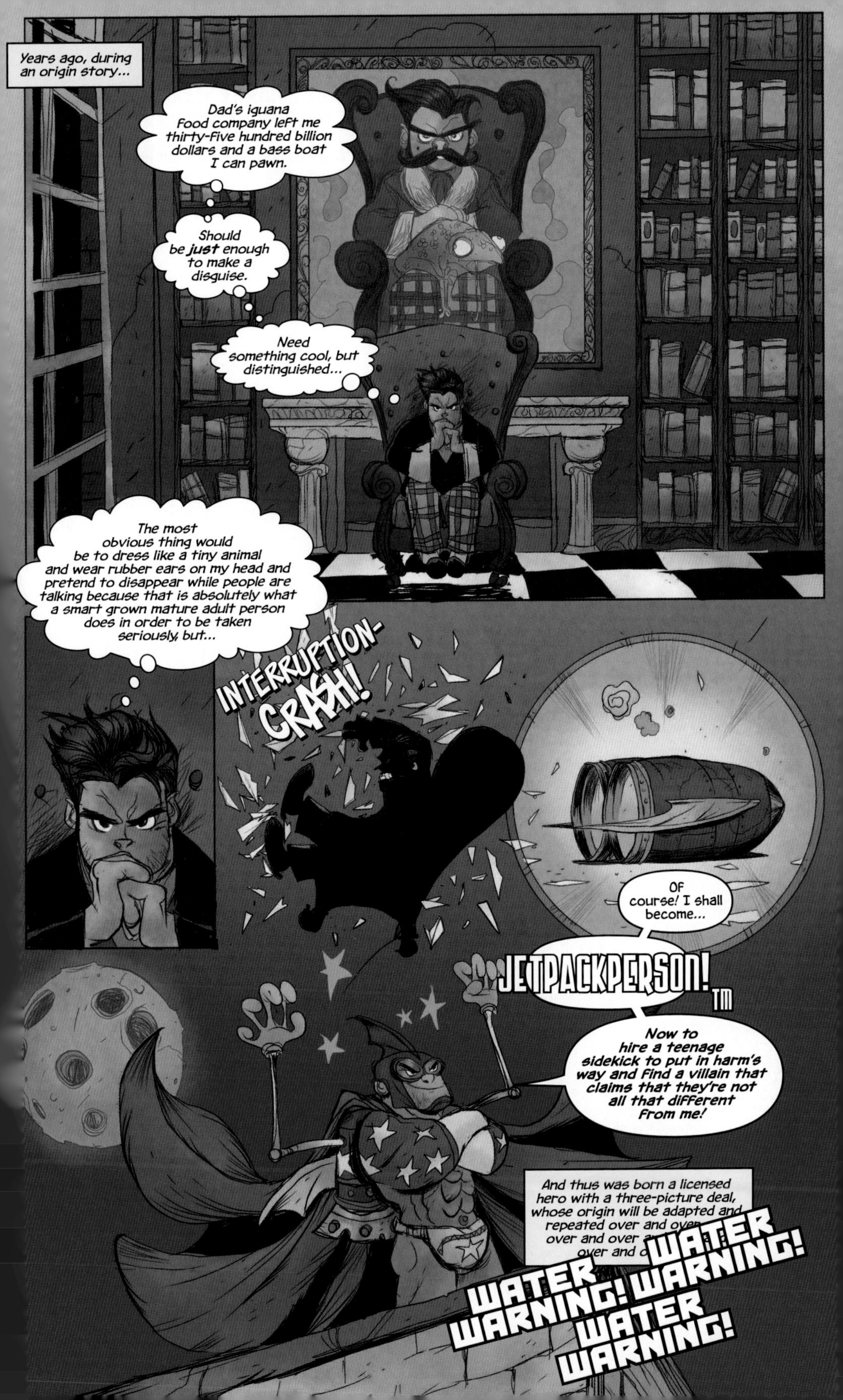

Years ago, during an origin story...
Dad's iguana food company left me thirty-five hundred billion dollars and a bass boat I can pawn.
Should be *just* enough to make a disguise.
Need something cool, but distinguished...
The most obvious thing would be to dress like a tiny animal and wear rubber ears on my head and pretend to disappear while people are talking because that is absolutely what a smart grown mature adult person does in order to be taken seriously, but...
INTERRUPTION-CRASH!
Of course! I shall become...
JETPACKPERSON! TM
Now to hire a teenage sidekick to put in harm's way and find a villain that claims that they're not all that different from me!
And thus was born a licensed hero with a three-picture deal, whose origin will be adapted and repeated over and over
WATER WARNING!
WATER WARNING!
WATER WARNING!

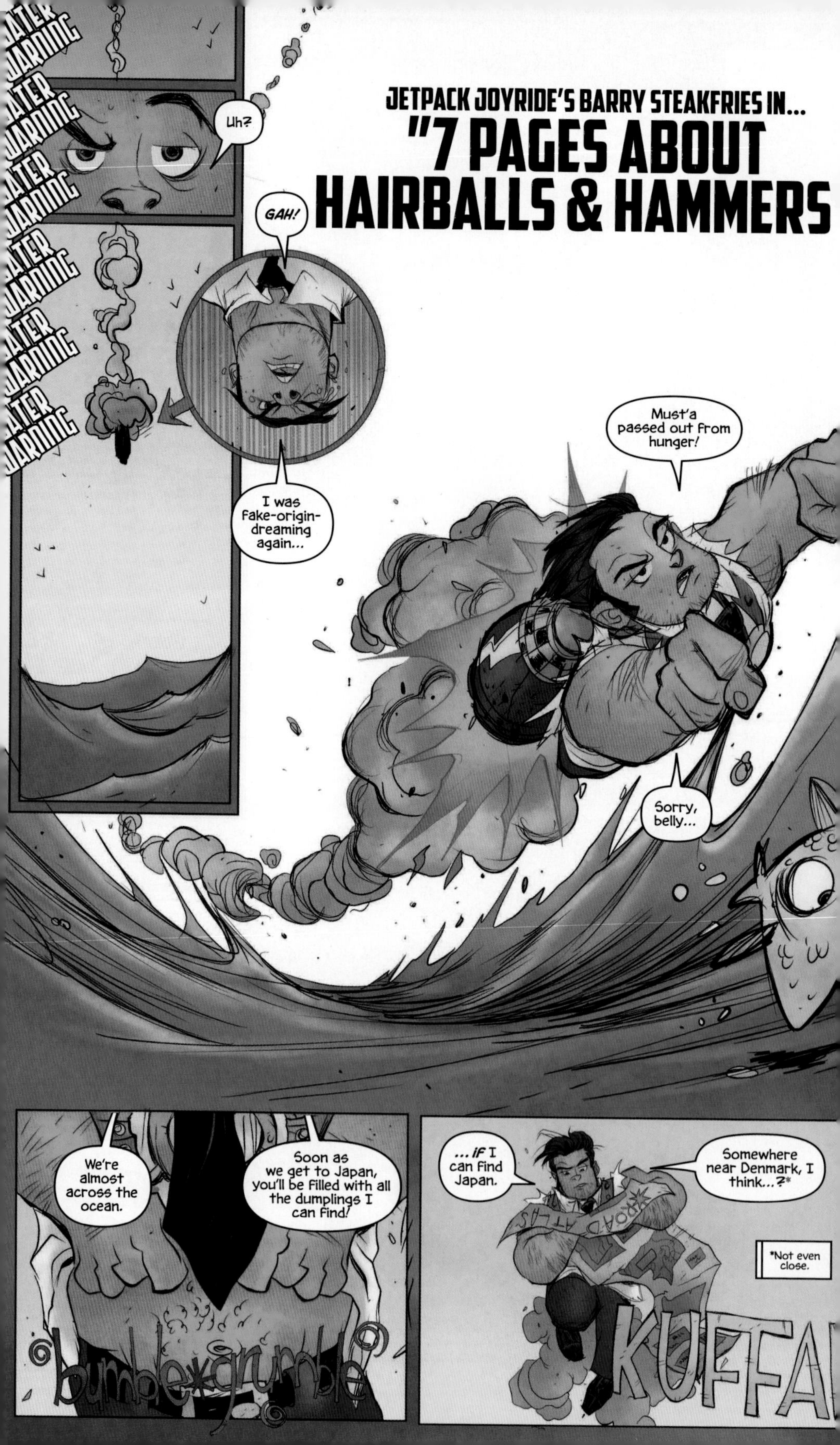
JETPACK JOYRIDE'S BARRY STEAKFRIES IN...
"7 PAGES ABOUT HAIRBALLS & HAMMERS
Uh?
GAH!
I was fake-origin-dreaming again...
Must'a passed out from hunger!
Sorry, belly...
We're almost across the ocean.
Soon as we get to Japan, you'll be filled with all the dumplings I can find!
bumble*grumble
...IF I can find Japan.
Somewhere near Denmark, I think...?*
ROAD ATLAS
*Not even close.
KUFFA

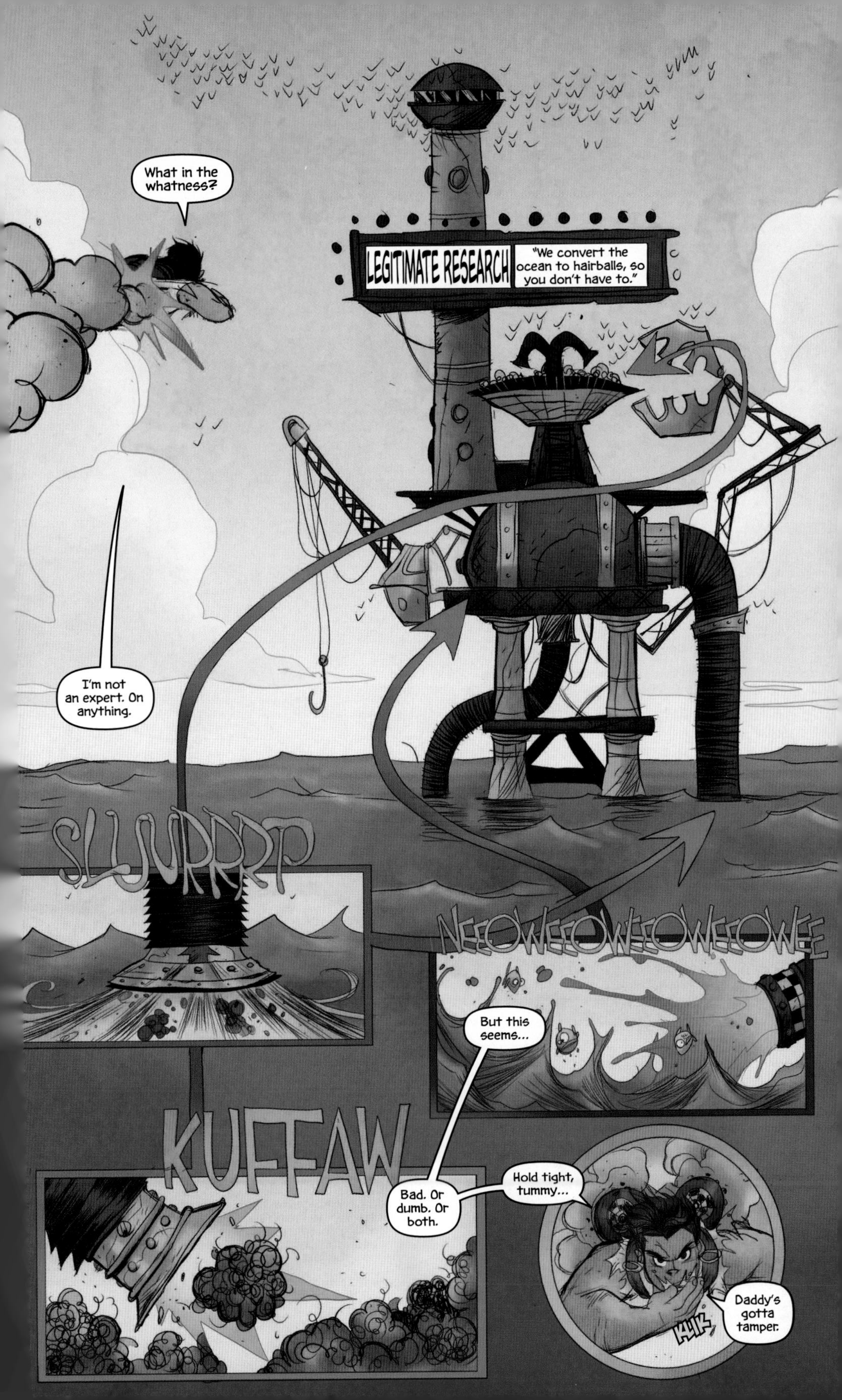
What in the whatness?
LEGITIMATE RESEARCH
"We convert the ocean to hairballs, so you don't have to."
I'm not an expert. On anything.
SLUURRRP
NEEOWEEOWEEOWEEOWEE
But this seems...
KUFFAW
Bad. Or dumb. Or both.
Hold tight, tummy...
Daddy's gotta tamper.

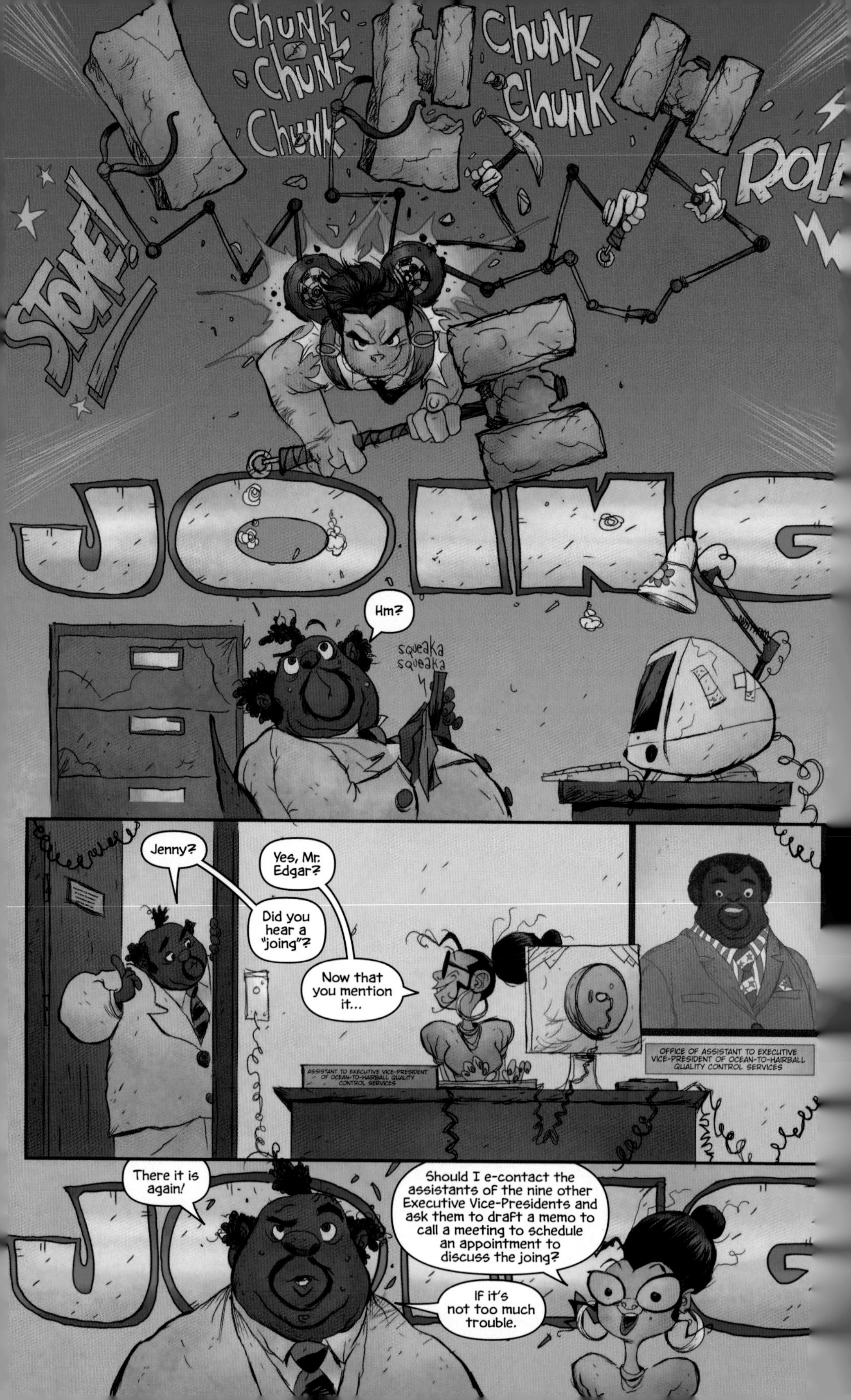

Chunk
Chunk
Chunk
Chunk
Chunk
STONE!
JOING
Hm?
squeaka squeaka
Jenny?
Did you hear a "joing"?
Yes, Mr. Edgar?
Now that you mention it...
ASSISTANT TO EXECUTIVE VICE-PRESIDENT OF OCEAN-TO-HAIRBALL QUALITY CONTROL SERVICES
OFFICE OF ASSISTANT TO EXECUTIVE VICE-PRESIDENT OF OCEAN-TO-HAIRBALL QUALITY CONTROL SERVICES
There it is again!
Should I e-contact the assistants of the nine other Executive Vice-Presidents and ask them to draft a memo to call a meeting to schedule an appointment to discuss the joing?
If it's not too much trouble.

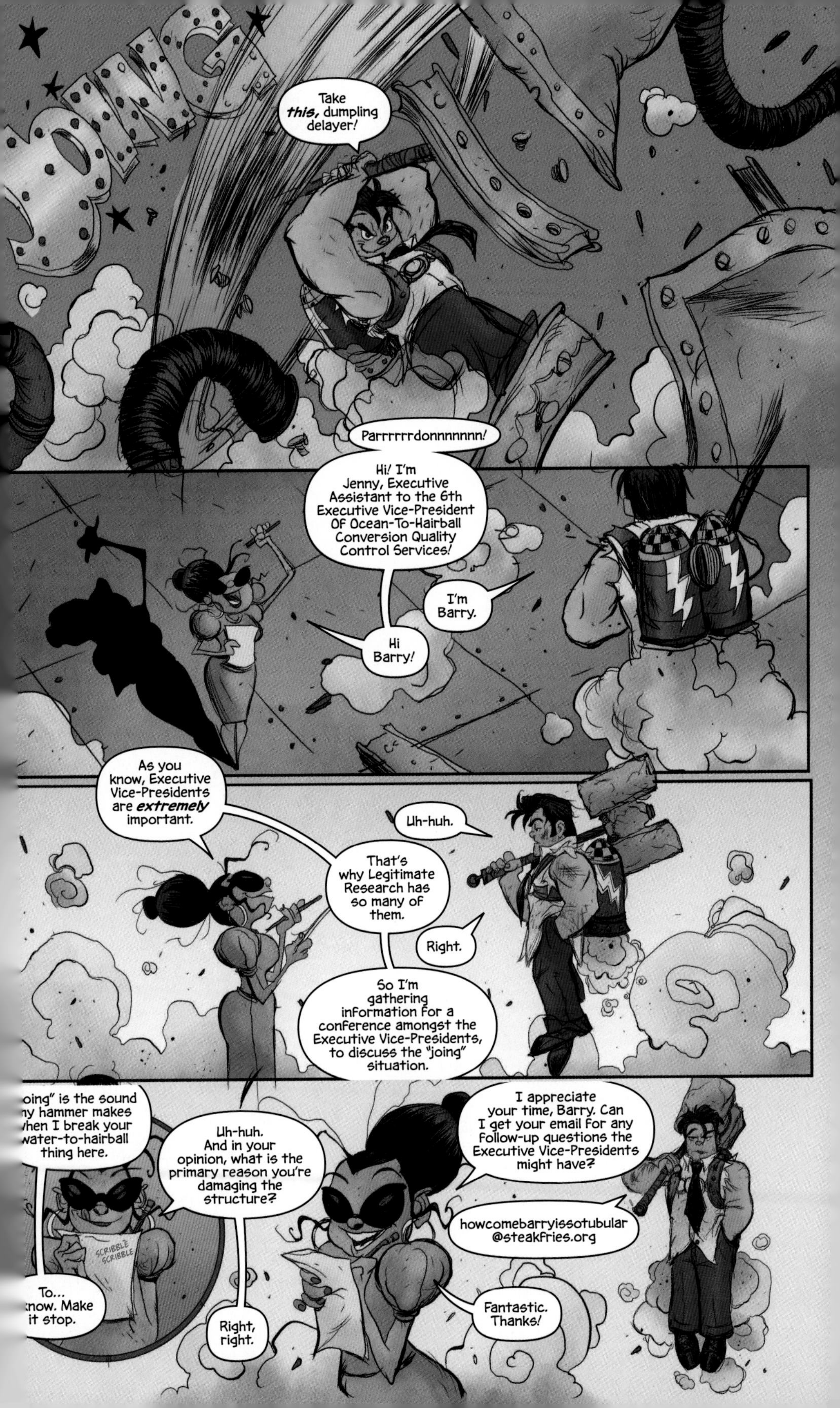
JOING!
Take *this,* dumpling delayer!
Parrrrrrdonnnnnnn!
Hi! I'm Jenny, Executive Assistant to the 6th Executive Vice-President Of Ocean-To-Hairball Conversion Quality Control Services!
I'm Barry.
Hi Barry!
As you know, Executive Vice-Presidents are *extremely* important.
Uh-huh.
That's why Legitimate Research has so many of them.
Right.
So I'm gathering information for a conference amongst the Executive Vice-Presidents, to discuss the "joing" situation.
oing" is the sound ny hammer makes hen I break your water-to-hairball thing here.
To... now. Make it stop.
Uh-huh. And in your opinion, what is the primary reason you're damaging the structure?
Right, right.
SCRIBBLE SCRIBBLE
I appreciate your time, Barry. Can I get your email for any follow-up questions the Executive Vice-Presidents might have?
howcomebarryissotubular @steakfries.org
Fantastic. Thanks!

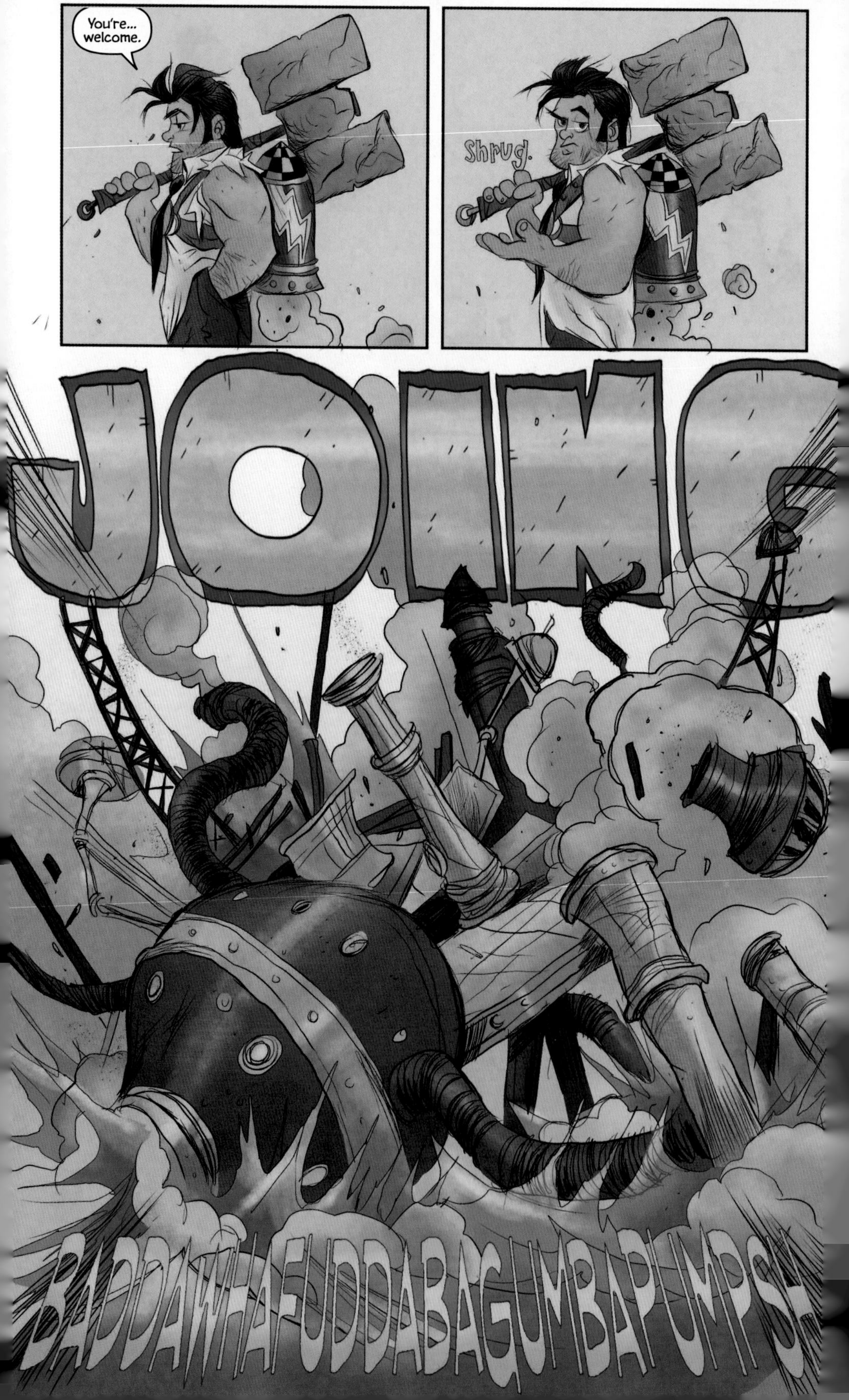

You're... welcome.
Shrug.
JOING
BADDAWHAFUDDABAGUMBAPUMPSH

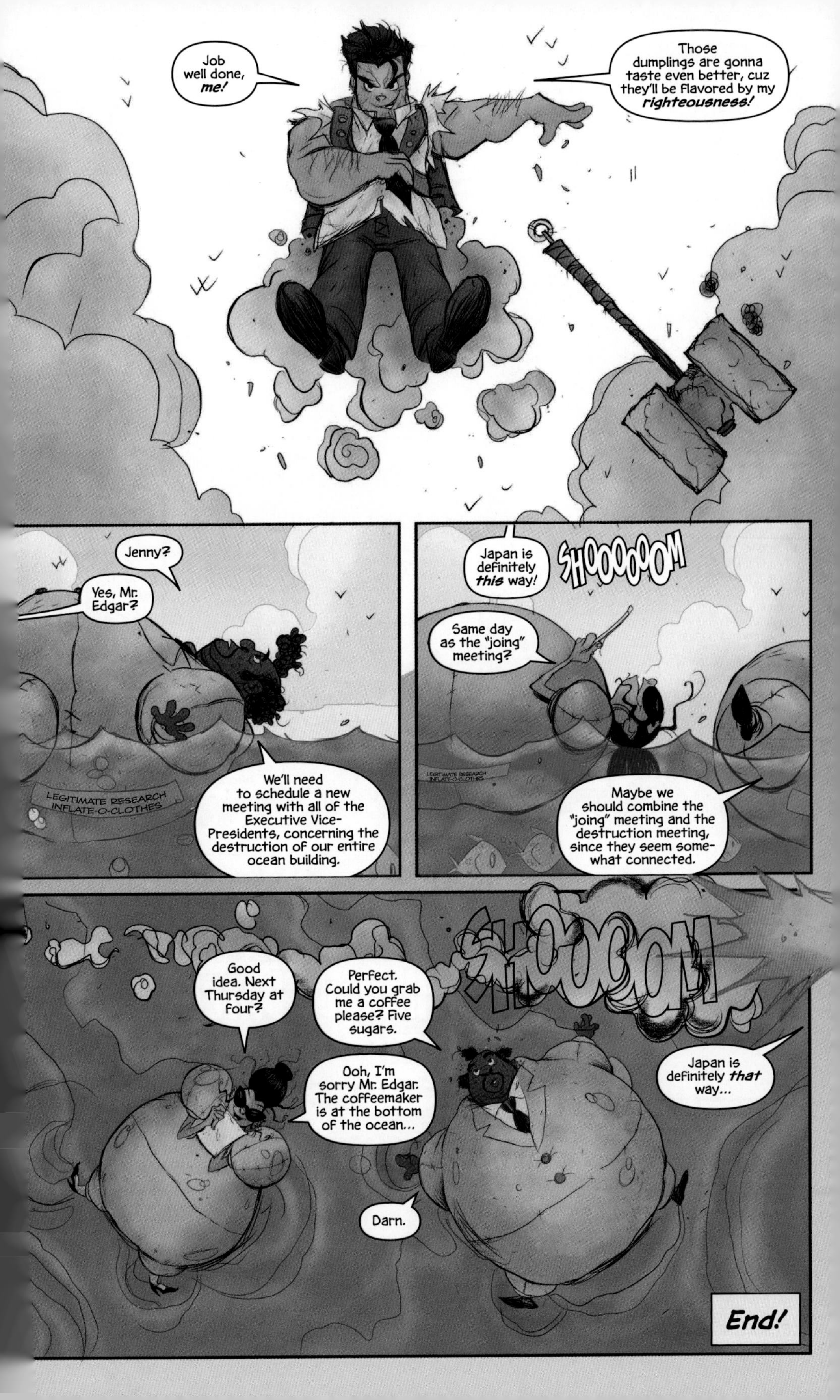
Job well done, *me!*
Those dumplings are gonna taste even better, cuz they'll be flavored by my *righteousness!*
Jenny?
Yes, Mr. Edgar?
LEGITIMATE RESEARCH INFLATE-O-CLOTHES
We'll need to schedule a new meeting with all of the Executive Vice-Presidents, concerning the destruction of our entire ocean building.
Japan is definitely *this* way!
SHOOOOOOM
Same day as the "joing" meeting?
LEGITIMATE RESEARCH INFLATE-O-CLOTHES
Maybe we should combine the "joing" meeting and the destruction meeting, since they seem some-what connected.
SHOOOOM
Good idea. Next Thursday at four?
Perfect. Could you grab me a coffee please? Five sugars.
Ooh, I'm sorry Mr. Edgar. The coffeemaker is at the bottom of the ocean...
Japan is definitely *that* way...
Darn.
End!

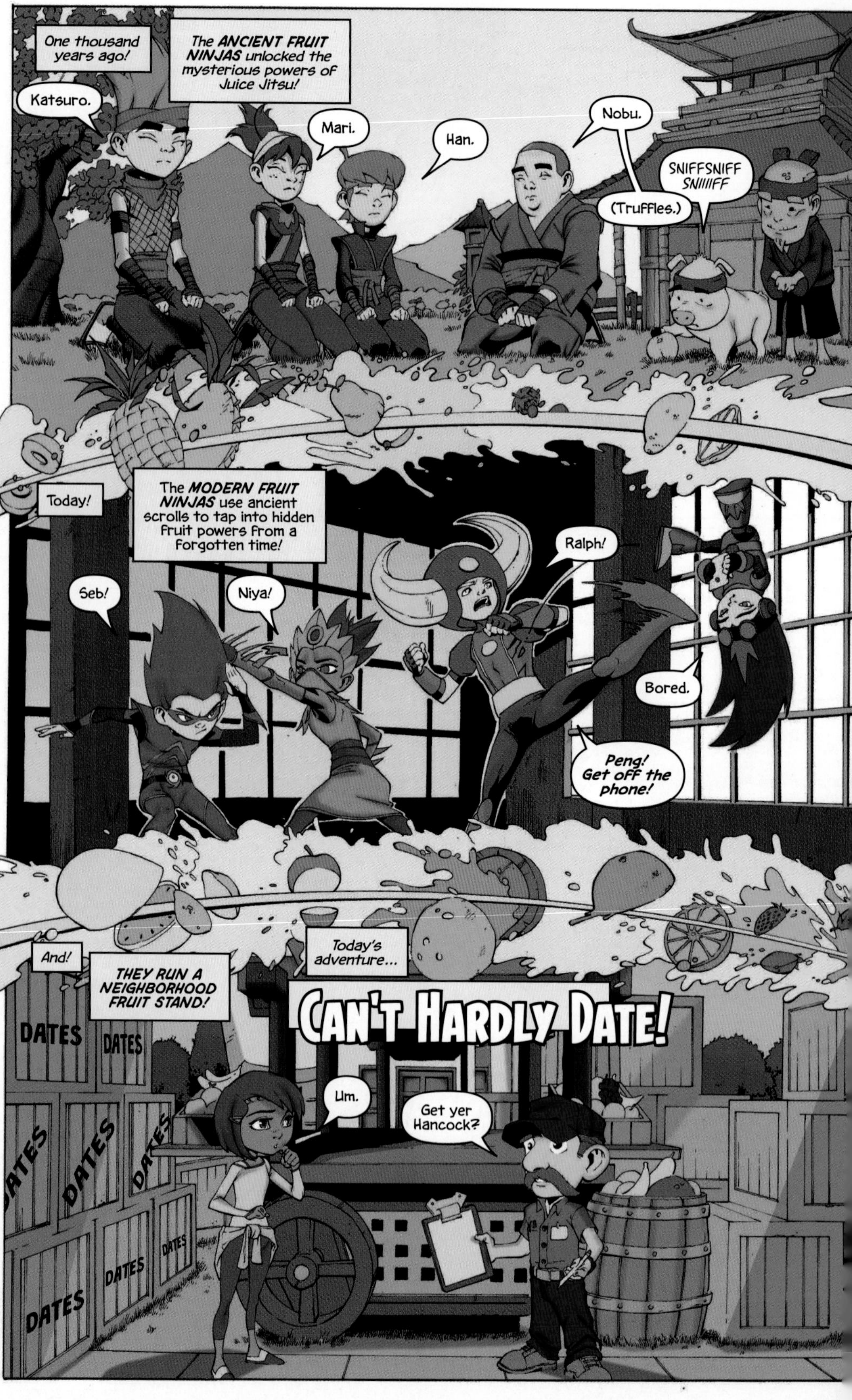

One thousand years ago!
The ANCIENT FRUIT NINJAS unlocked the mysterious powers of Juice Jitsu!
Katsuro.
Mari.
Han.
Nobu.
SNIFFSNIFF SNIIIIFF
(Truffles.)
Today!
The MODERN FRUIT NINJAS use ancient scrolls to tap into hidden fruit powers from a forgotten time!
Ralph!
Seb!
Niya!
Bored.
Peng! Get off the phone!
And!
THEY RUN A NEIGHBORHOOD FRUIT STAND!
Today's adventure...
CAN'T HARDLY DATE!
DATES
Um.
Get yer Hancock?

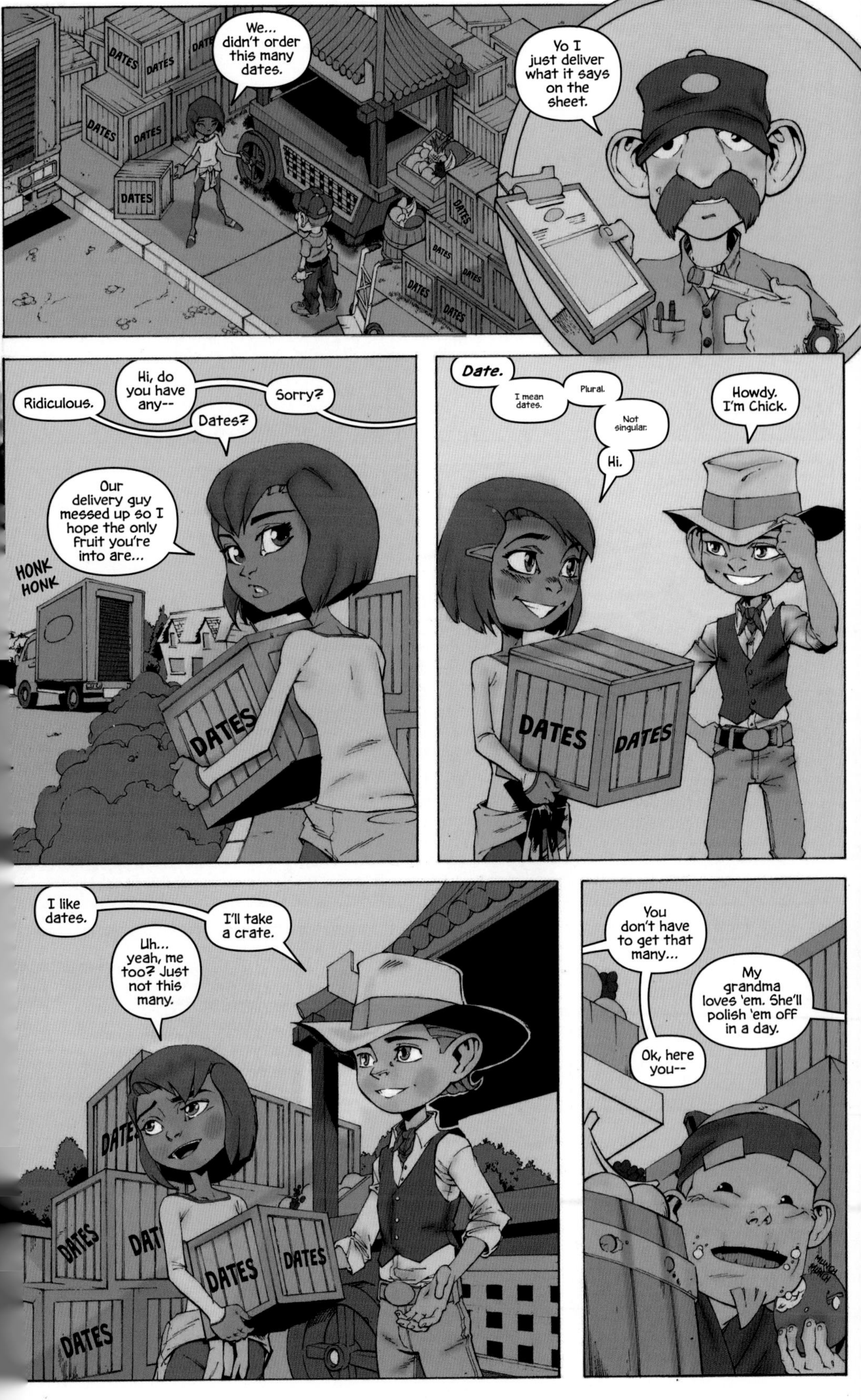

We... didn't order this many dates.
Yo I just deliver what it says on the sheet.
Ridiculous.
Hi, do you have any--
Dates?
Sorry?
Our delivery guy messed up so I hope the only fruit you're into are...
HONK HONK
Date.
I mean dates.
Plural.
Not singular.
Hi.
Howdy. I'm Chick.
I like dates.
I'll take a crate.
Uh... yeah, me too? Just not this many.
You don't have to get that many...
My grandma loves 'em. She'll polish 'em off in a day.
Ok, here you--
MUNCH MUNCH

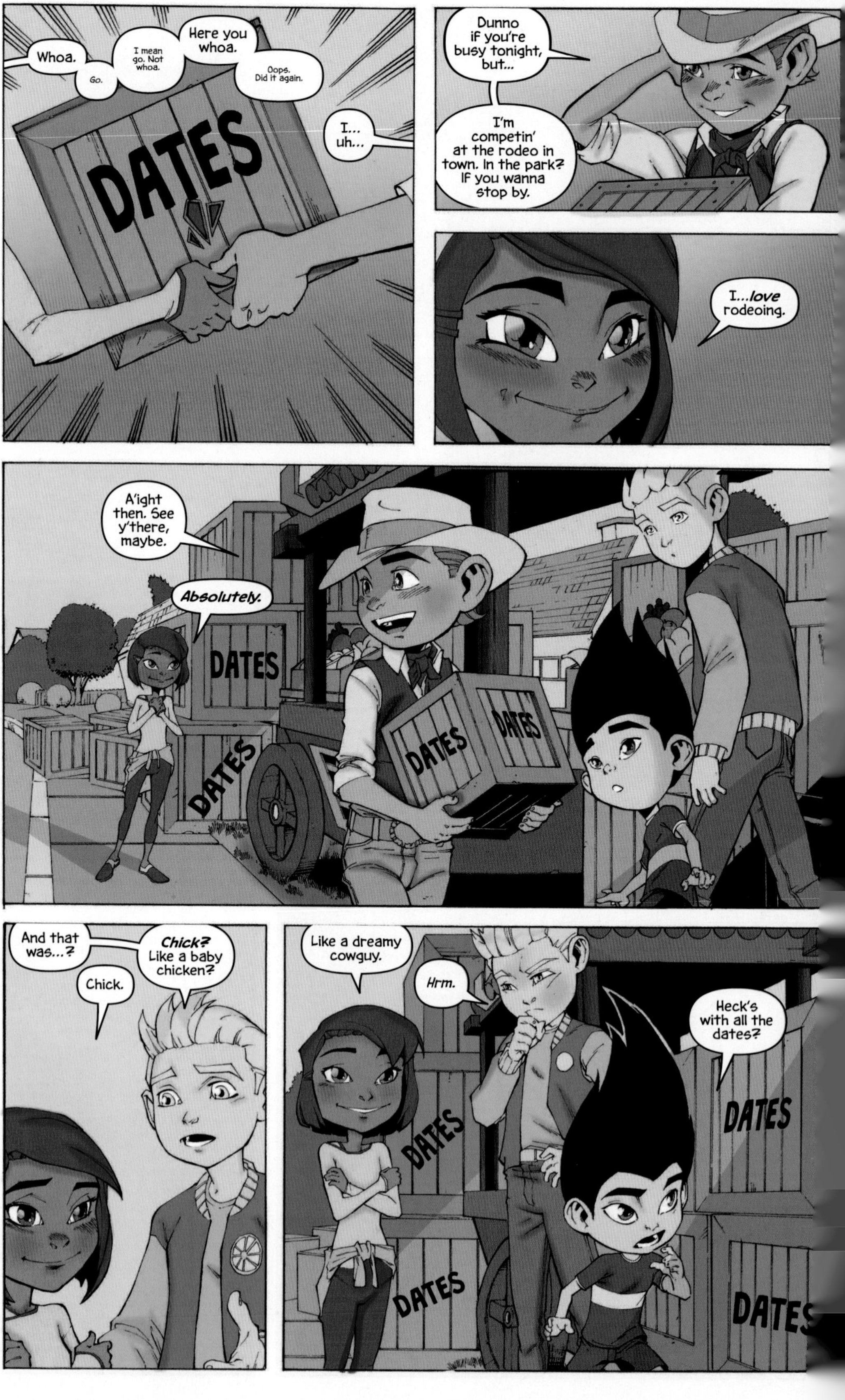

Whoa.
Go.
I mean go. Not whoa.
Here you whoa.
Oops. Did it again.
I... uh...
DATES
Dunno if you're busy tonight, but...
I'm competin' at the rodeo in town. In the park? If you wanna stop by.
I...*love* rodeoing.
A'ight then. See y'there, maybe.
Absolutely.
DATES
DATES
DATES
DATES
And that was...?
Chick.
Chick? Like a baby chicken?
Like a dreamy cowguy.
Hrm.
Heck's with all the dates?
DATES
DATES
DATES
DATES

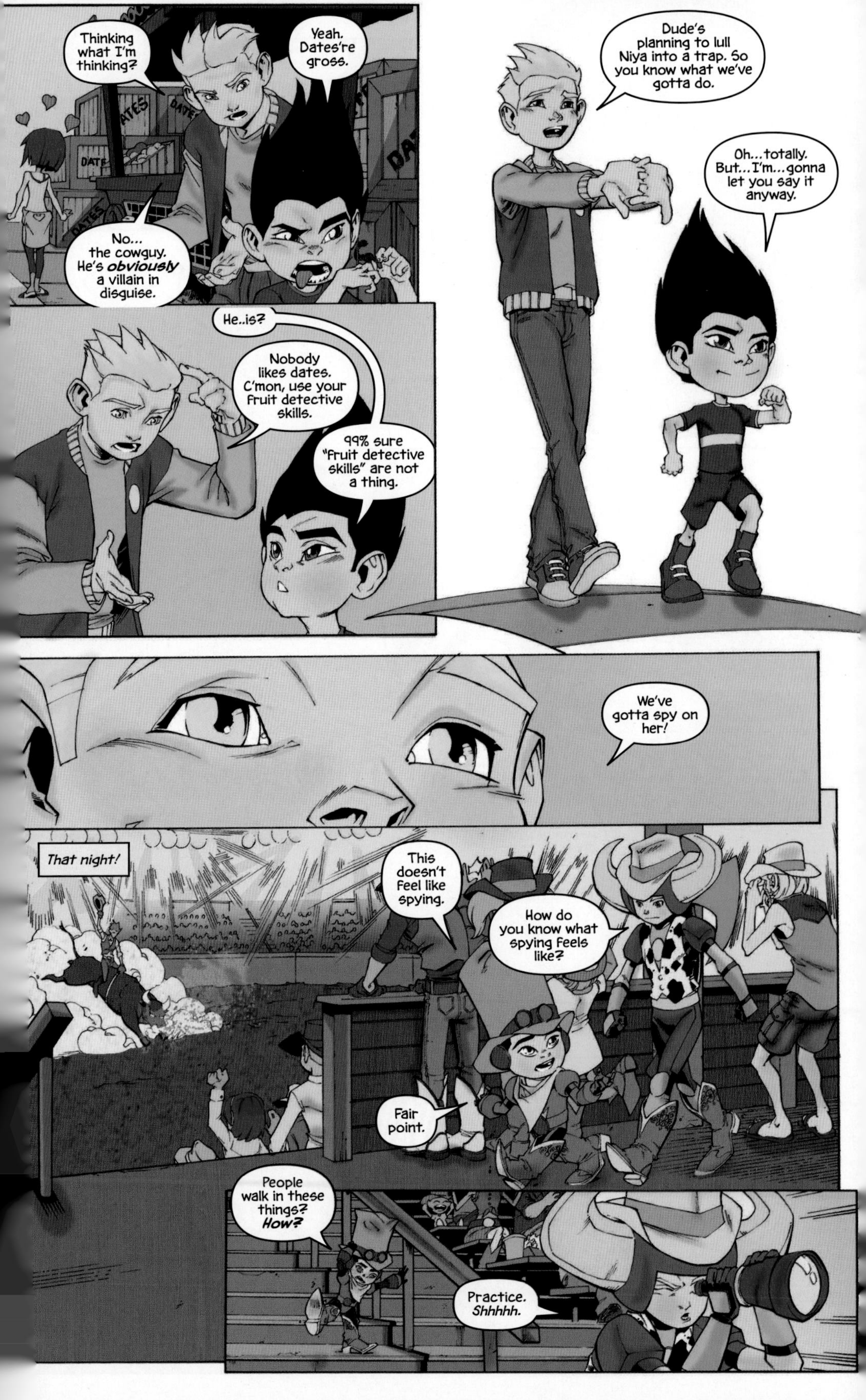

Thinking what I'm thinking?
Yeah. Dates're gross.
No... the cowguy. He's ***obviously*** a villain in disguise.
Dude's planning to lull Niya into a trap. So you know what we've gotta do.
Oh...totally. But...I'm...gonna let you say it anyway.
He..is?
Nobody likes dates. C'mon, use your fruit detective skills.
99% sure "fruit detective skills" are not a thing.
We've gotta spy on her!
That night!
This doesn't feel like spying.
How do you know what spying feels like?
Fair point.
People walk in these things? ***How?***
Practice. *Shhhhh.*

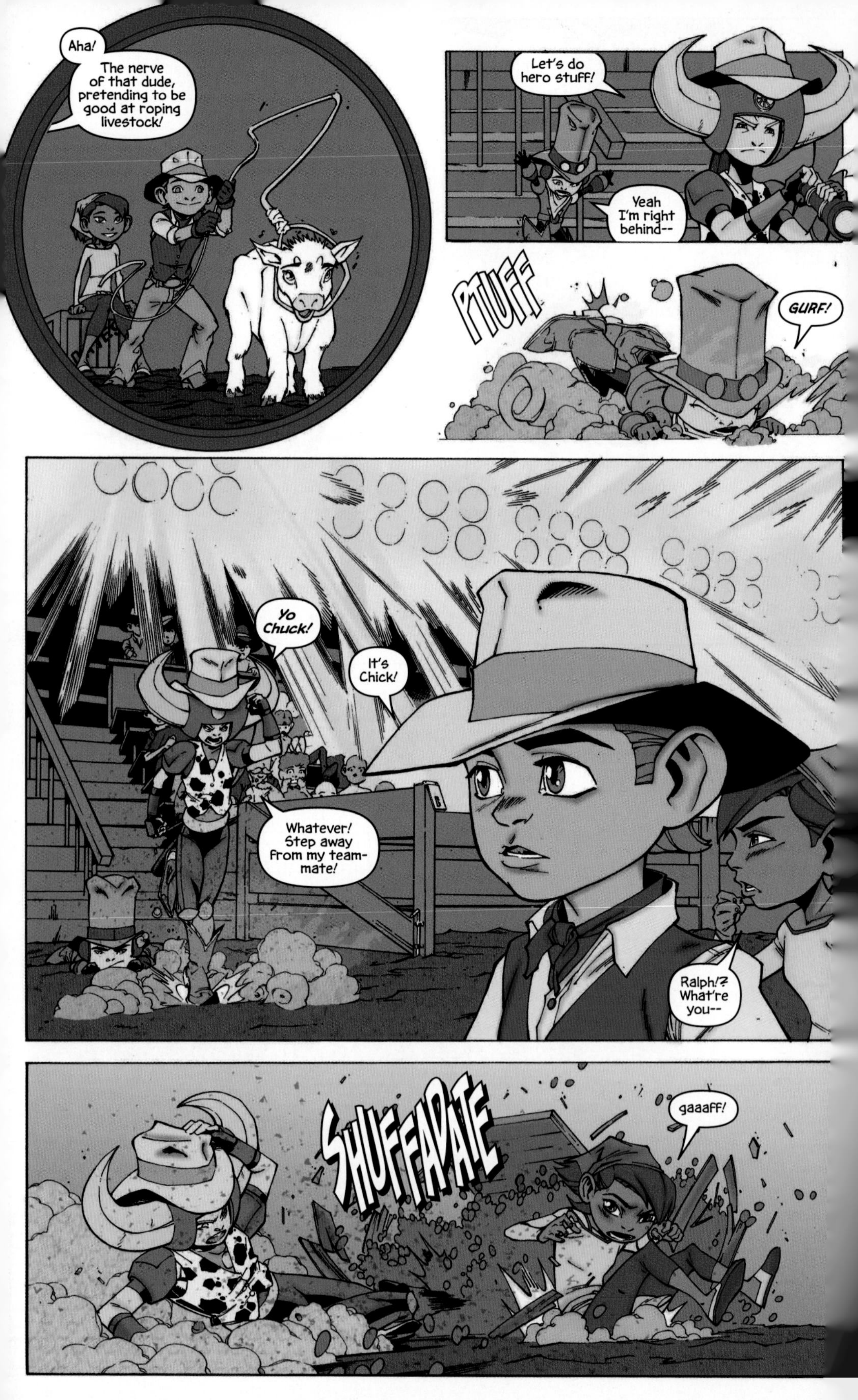
Aha!
The nerve of that dude, pretending to be good at roping livestock!
Let's do hero stuff!
Yeah I'm right behind--
PTTUFF
GURF!
Yo Chuck!
It's Chick!
Whatever! Step away from my team-mate!
Ralph!? What're you--
SHUFFAPATE
gaaaff!

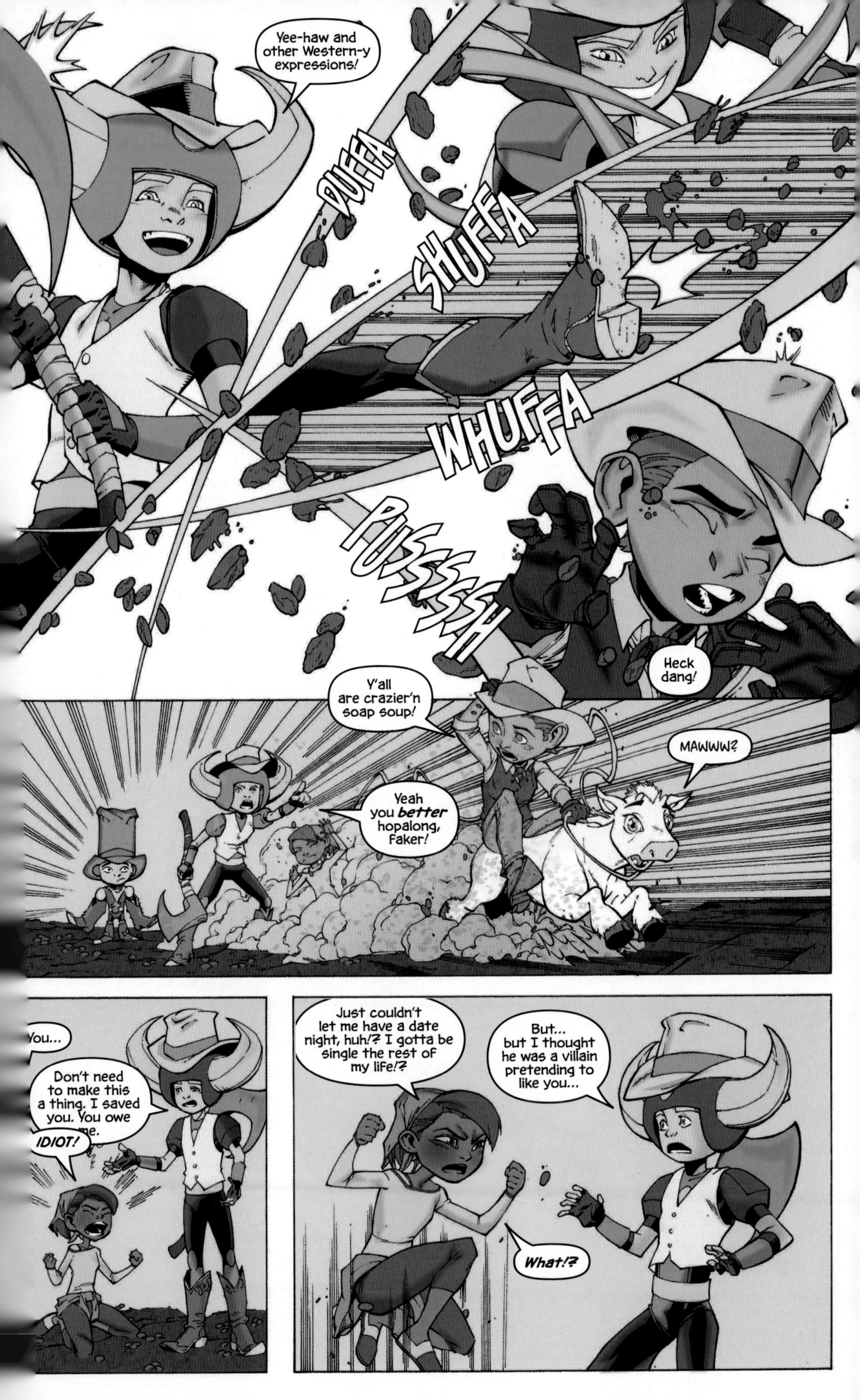

Yee-haw and other Western-y expressions!
DUFFA
SHUFFA
WHUFFA
PUSSSSH
Heck dang!
Y'all are crazier'n soap soup!
MAWWW?
Yeah you **better** hopalong, Faker!
You...
Don't need to make this a thing. I saved you. You owe me.
IDIOT!
Just couldn't let me have a date night, huh!? I gotta be single the rest of my life!?
But... but I thought he was a villain pretending to like you...
What!?

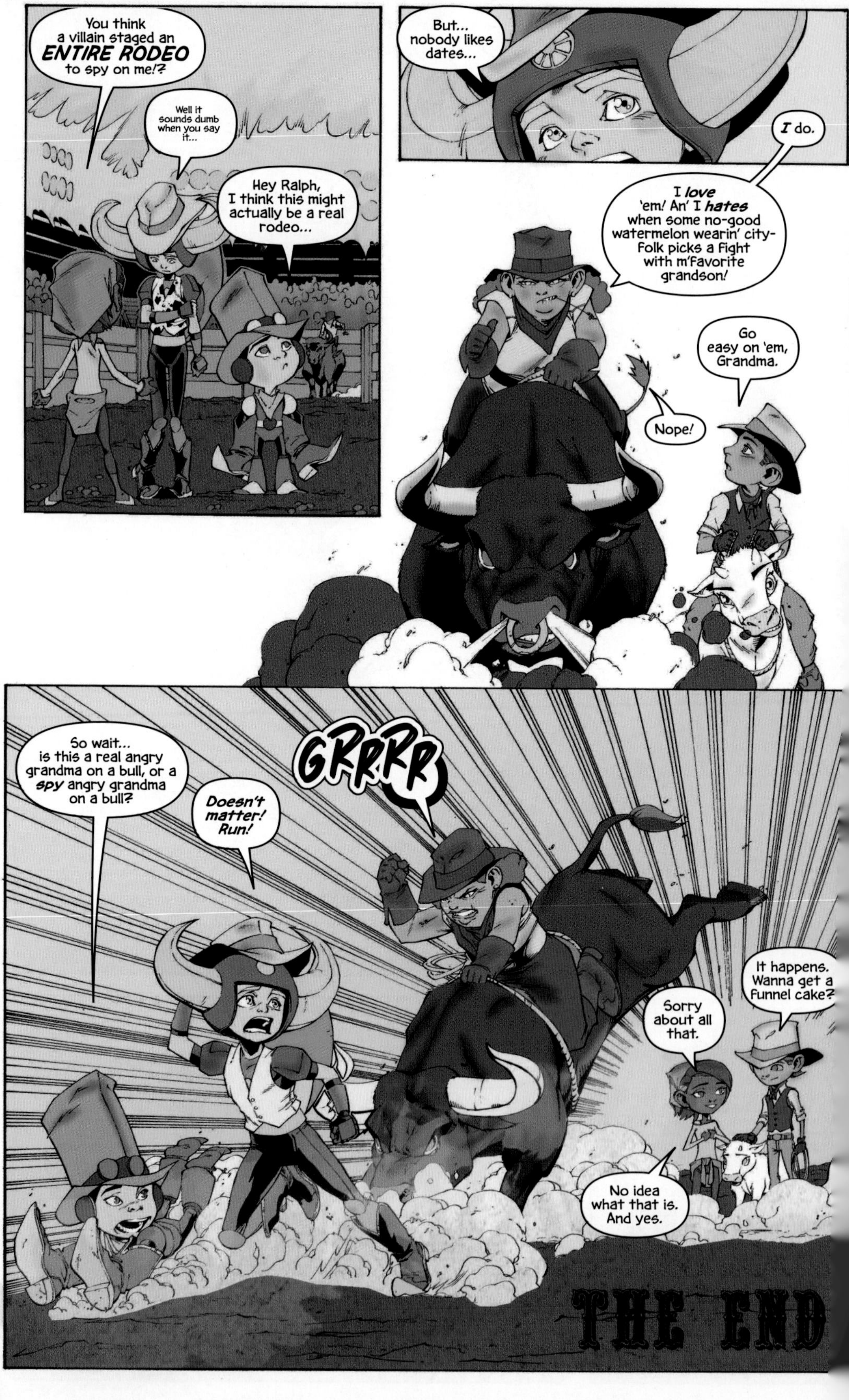
You think a villain staged an ENTIRE RODEO to spy on me!?
Well it sounds dumb when you say it...
Hey Ralph, I think this might actually be a real rodeo...
But... nobody likes dates...
I do.
I love 'em! An' I hates when some no-good watermelon wearin' city-folk picks a fight with m'favorite grandson!
Go easy on 'em, Grandma.
Nope!
So wait... is this a real angry grandma on a bull, or a spy angry grandma on a bull?
GRRRR
Doesn't matter! Run!
Sorry about all that.
It happens. Wanna get a funnel cake?
No idea what that is. And yes.
THE END

ART BY

SCOTT BROWN

COLORS BY

DEARBHLA KELLY

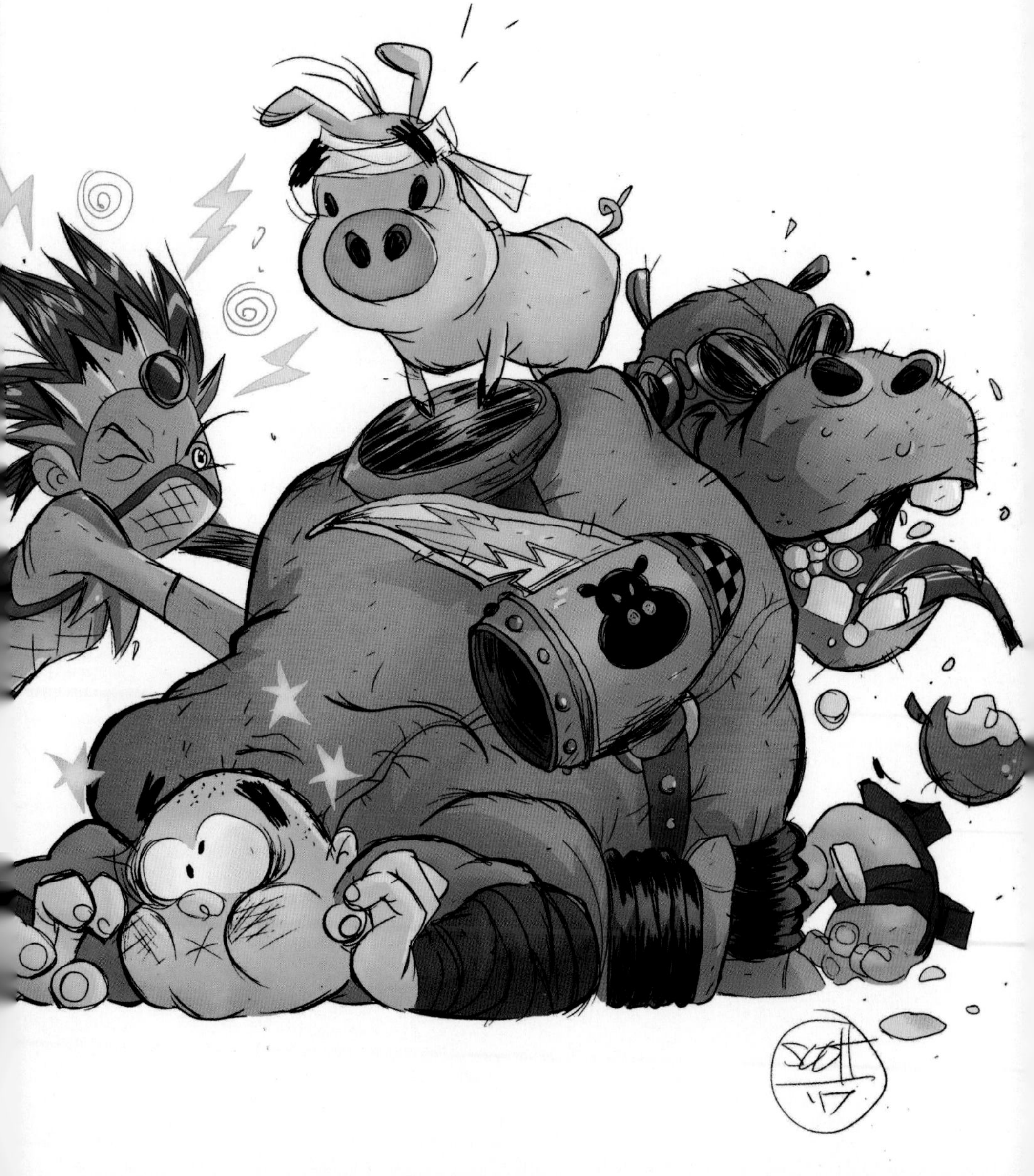

SCOTT
'17

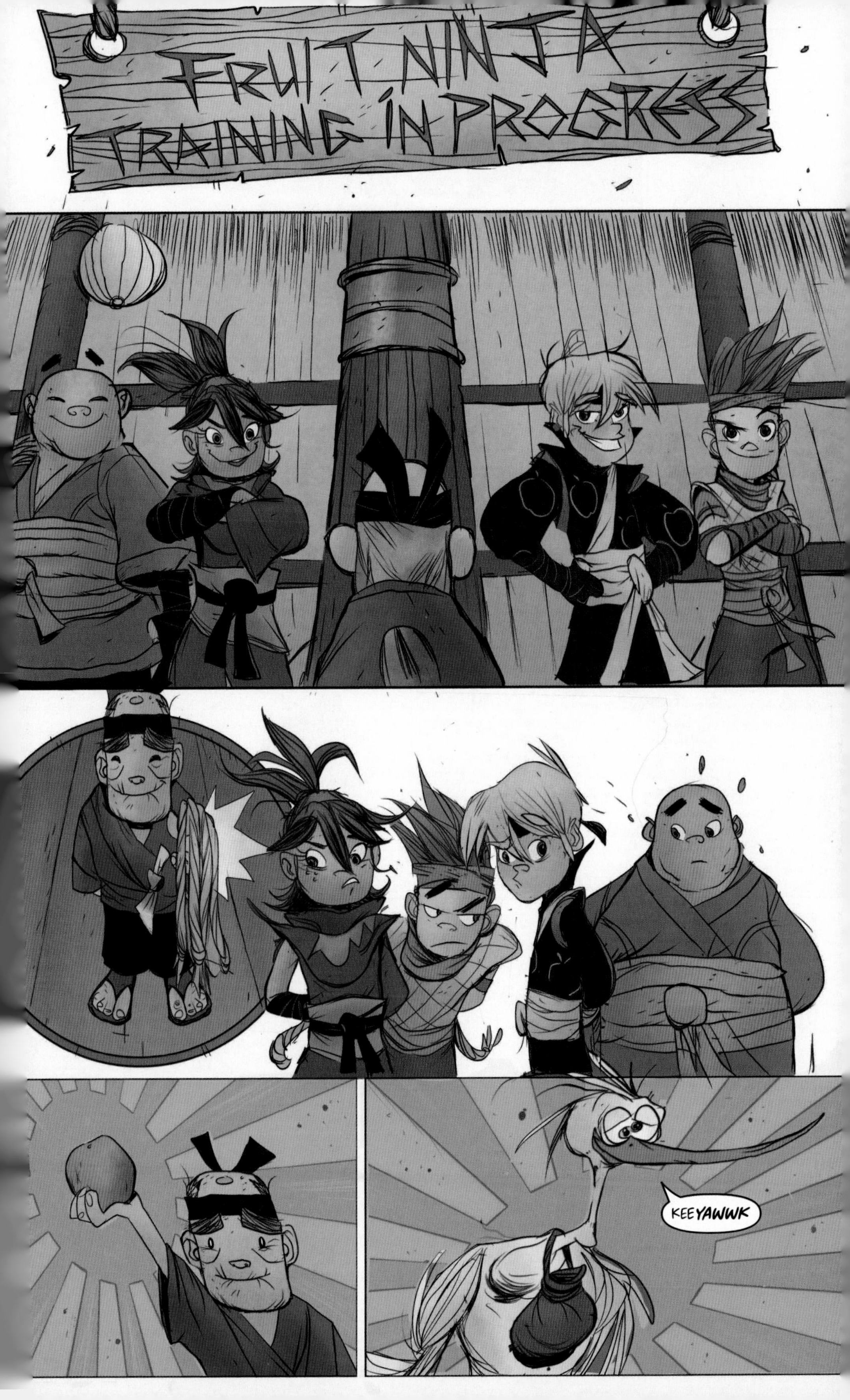
FRUIT NINJA TRAINING IN PROGRESS
KEEYAWWK

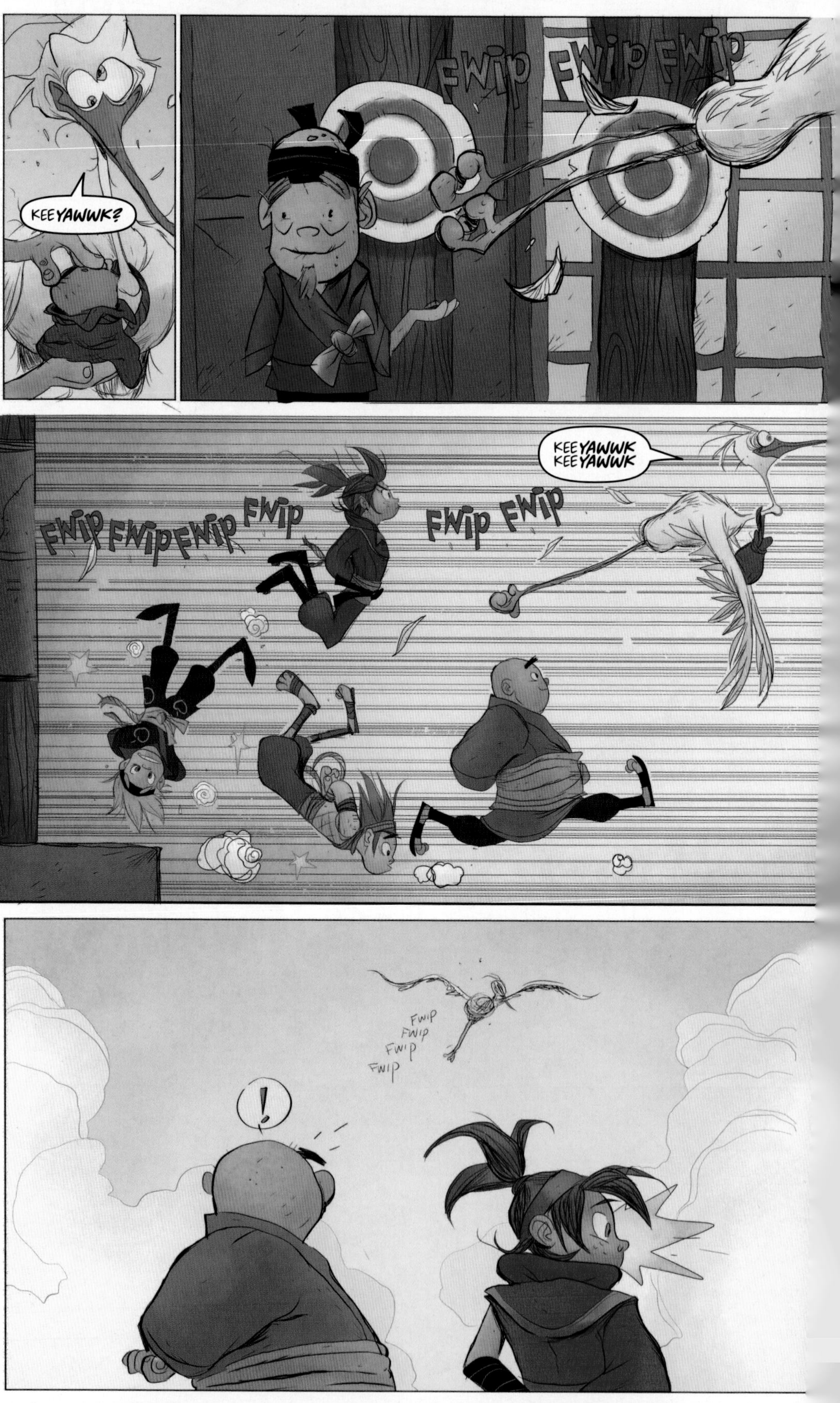
KEEYAWWK?
FWIP FWIP FWIP
KEEYAWWK
KEEYAWWK
FWIP FWIP FWIP FWIP
FWIP FWIP
FWIP
FWIP
FWIP
FWIP
!

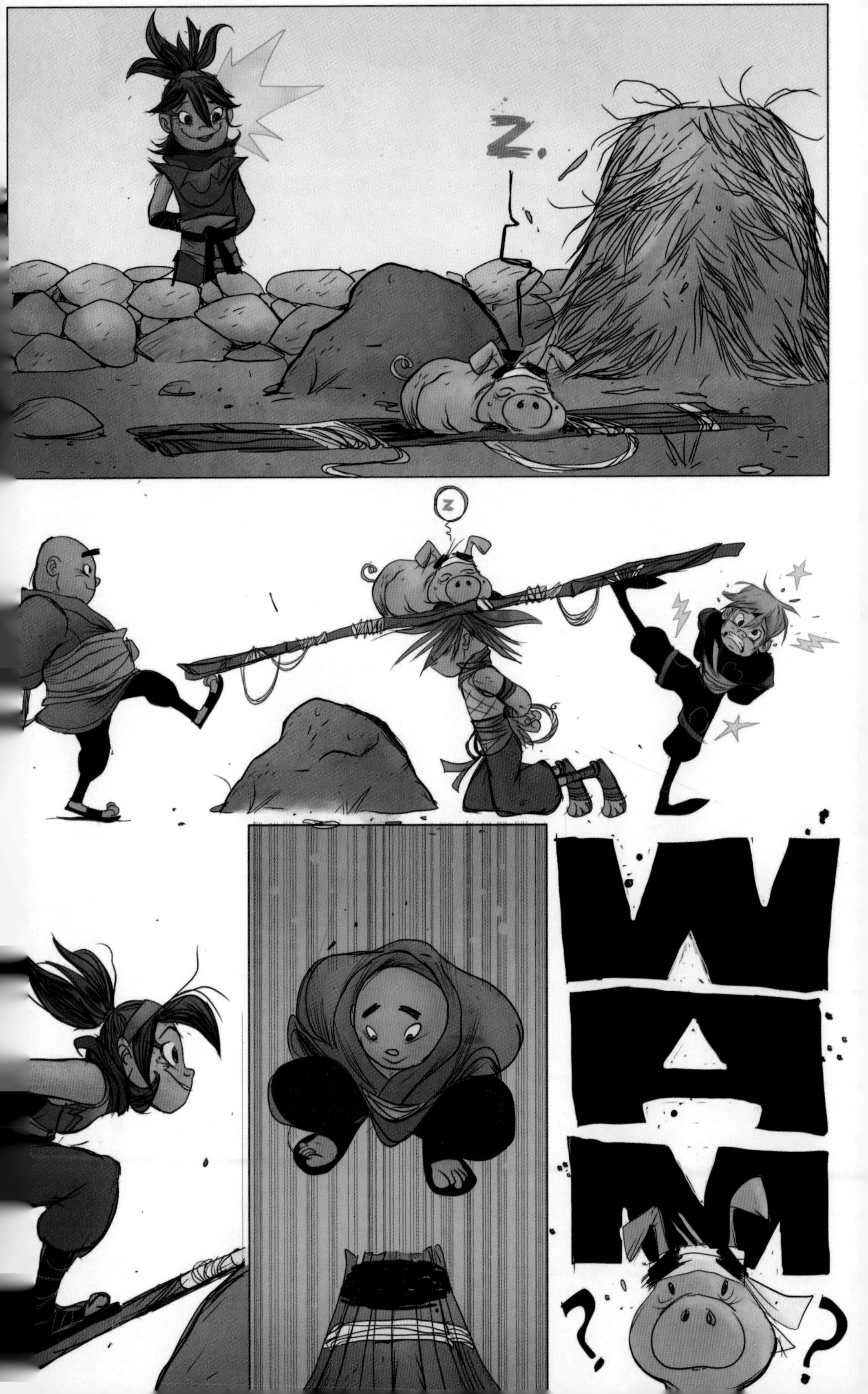
Z.
Z
WAM
? ?

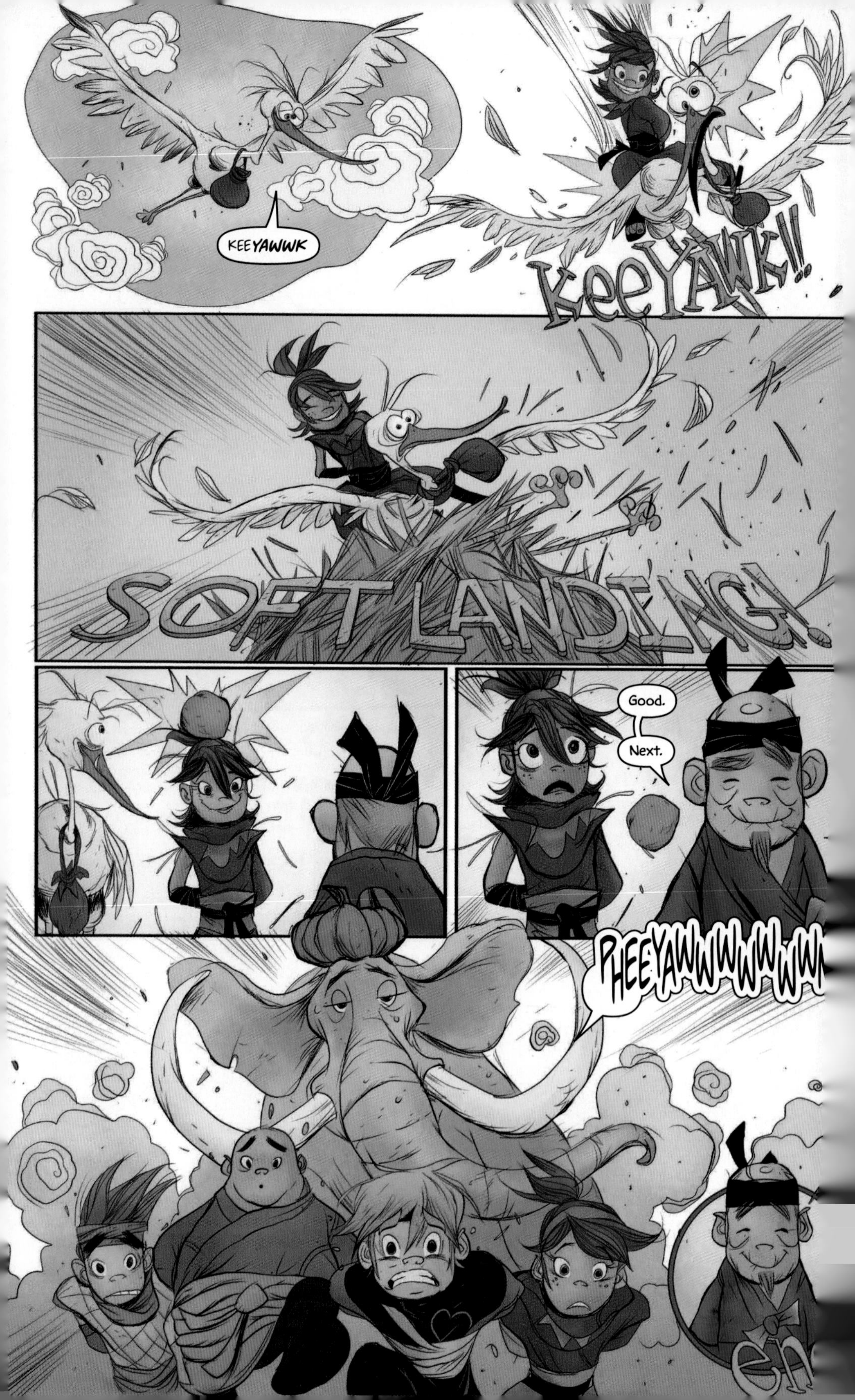
KEEYAWWK
KEEYAWK!!
SOFT LANDING!
Good.
Next.
PHEEYAWWWWWWWW

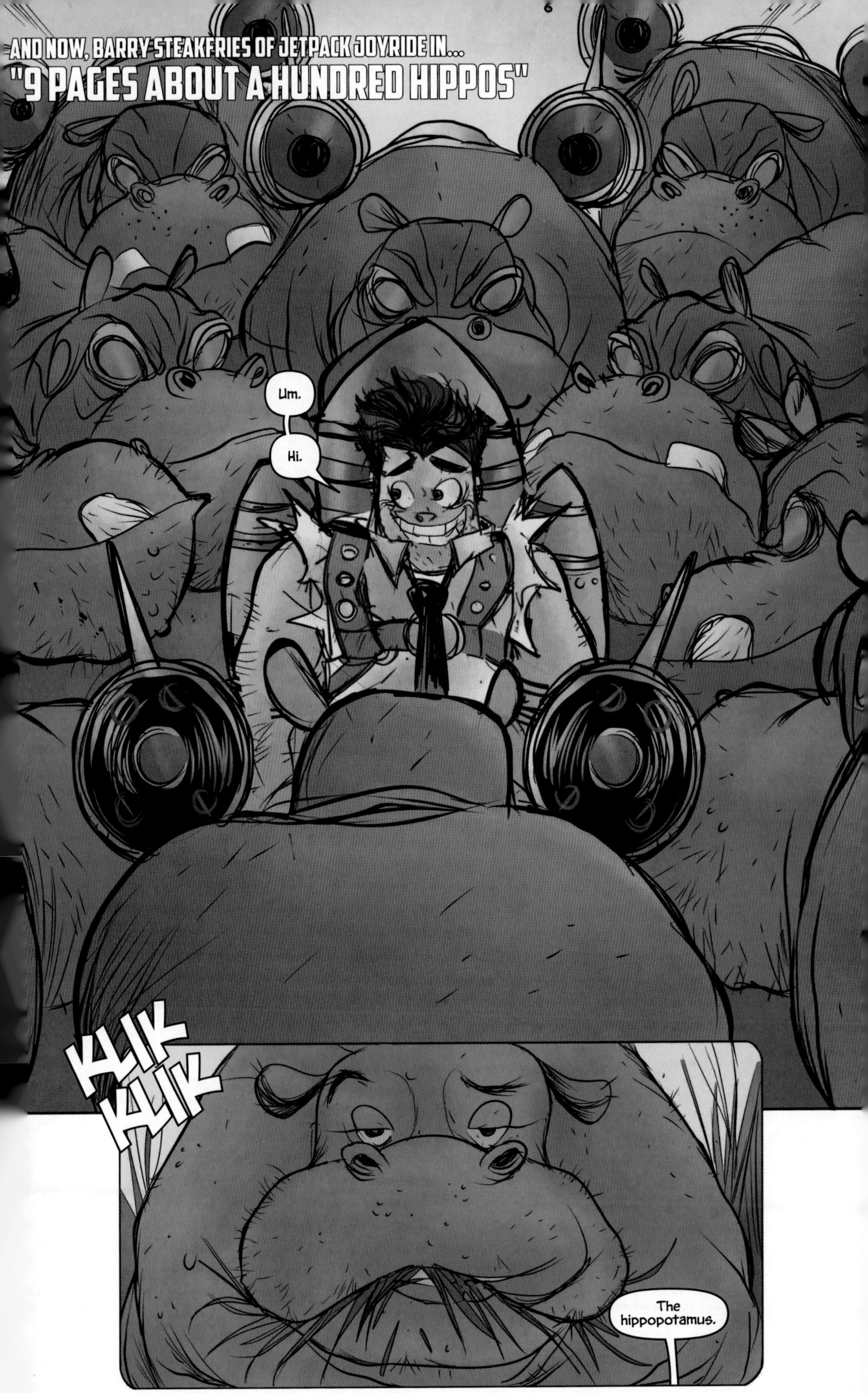
AND NOW, BARRY STEAKFRIES OF JETPACK JOYRIDE IN...
"9 PAGES ABOUT A HUNDRED HIPPOS"
Um.
Hi.
KLIK KLIK
The hippopotamus.

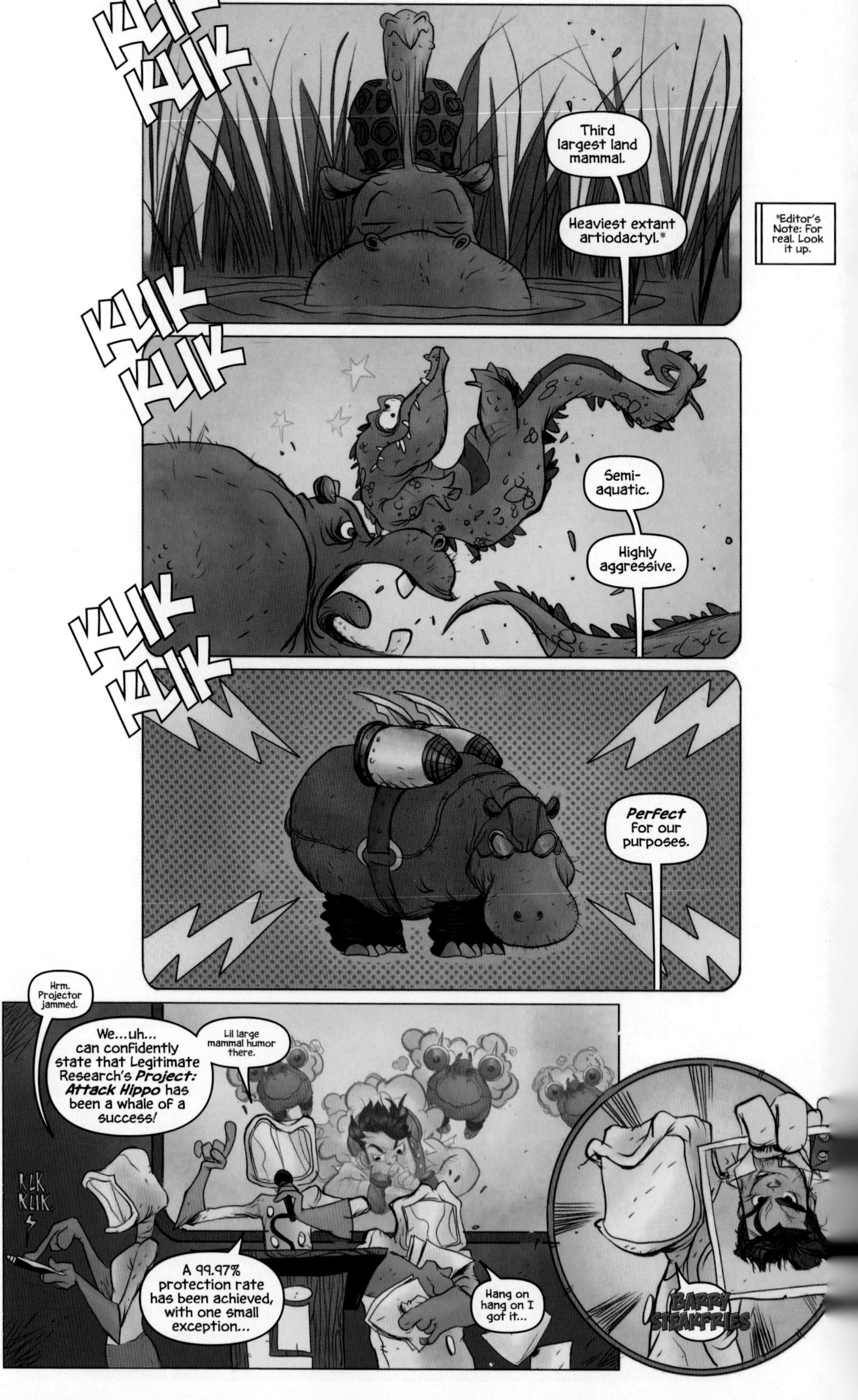
KLIK KLIK
Third largest land mammal.
Heaviest extant artiodactyl.*
*Editor's Note: For real. Look it up.
KLIK KLIK
Semi-aquatic.
Highly aggressive.
KLIK KLIK
Perfect for our purposes.
Hrm. Projector jammed.
We...uh... can confidently state that Legitimate Research's Project: Attack Hippo has been a whale of a success!
Lil large mammal humor there.
KLK KLIK.
A 99.97% protection rate has been achieved, with one small exception...
Hang on hang on I got it...
BARRY STEAKFRIES

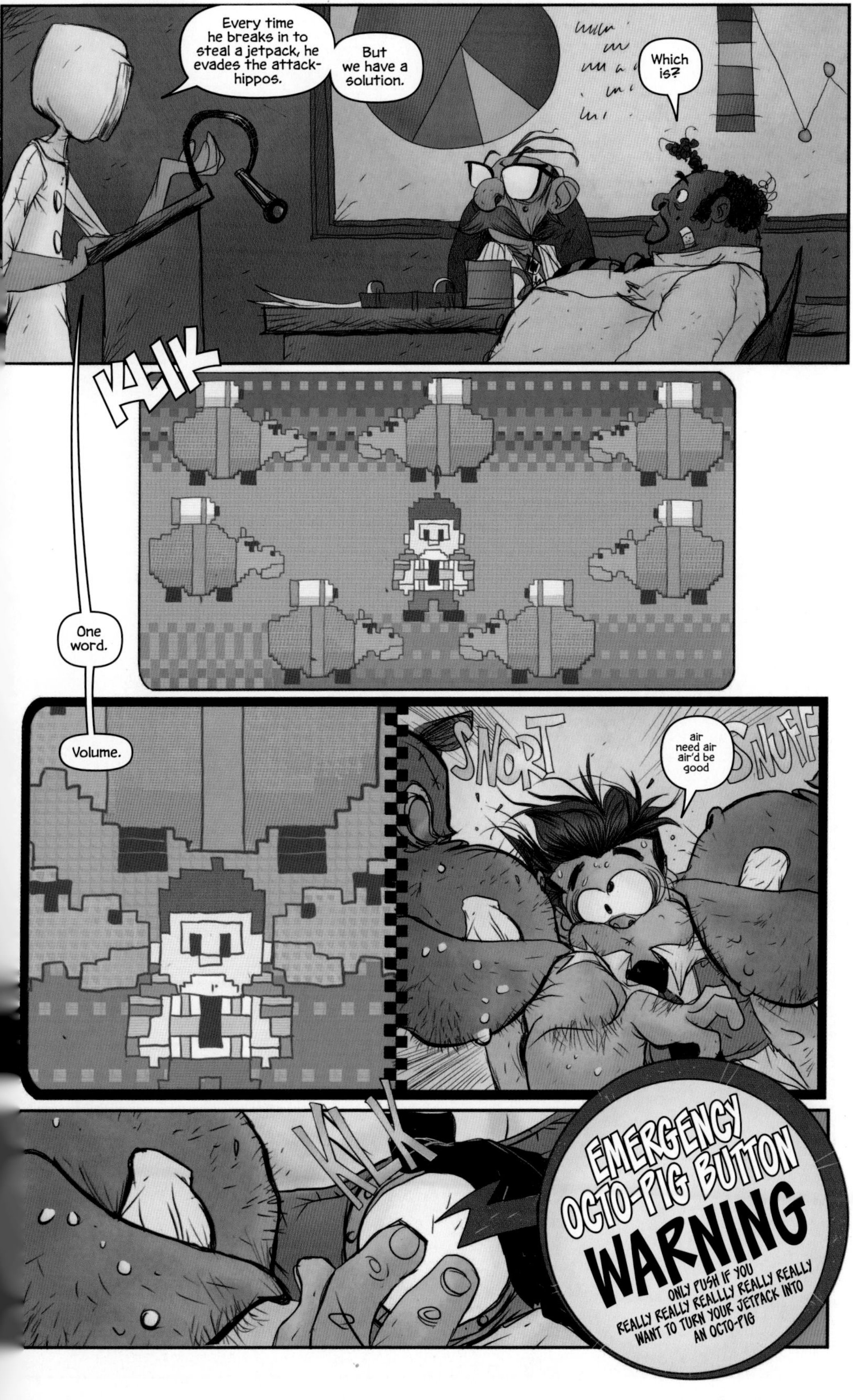
Every time he breaks in to steal a jetpack, he evades the attack-hippos.
But we have a solution.
Which is?
KLIK
One word.
Volume.
SNORT
SNUFF
air need air air'd be good
KLIK
EMERGENCY OCTO-PIG BUTTON
WARNING
ONLY PUSH IF YOU REALLY REALLY REALLLY REALLY REALLY WANT TO TURN YOUR JETPACK INTO AN OCTO-PIG

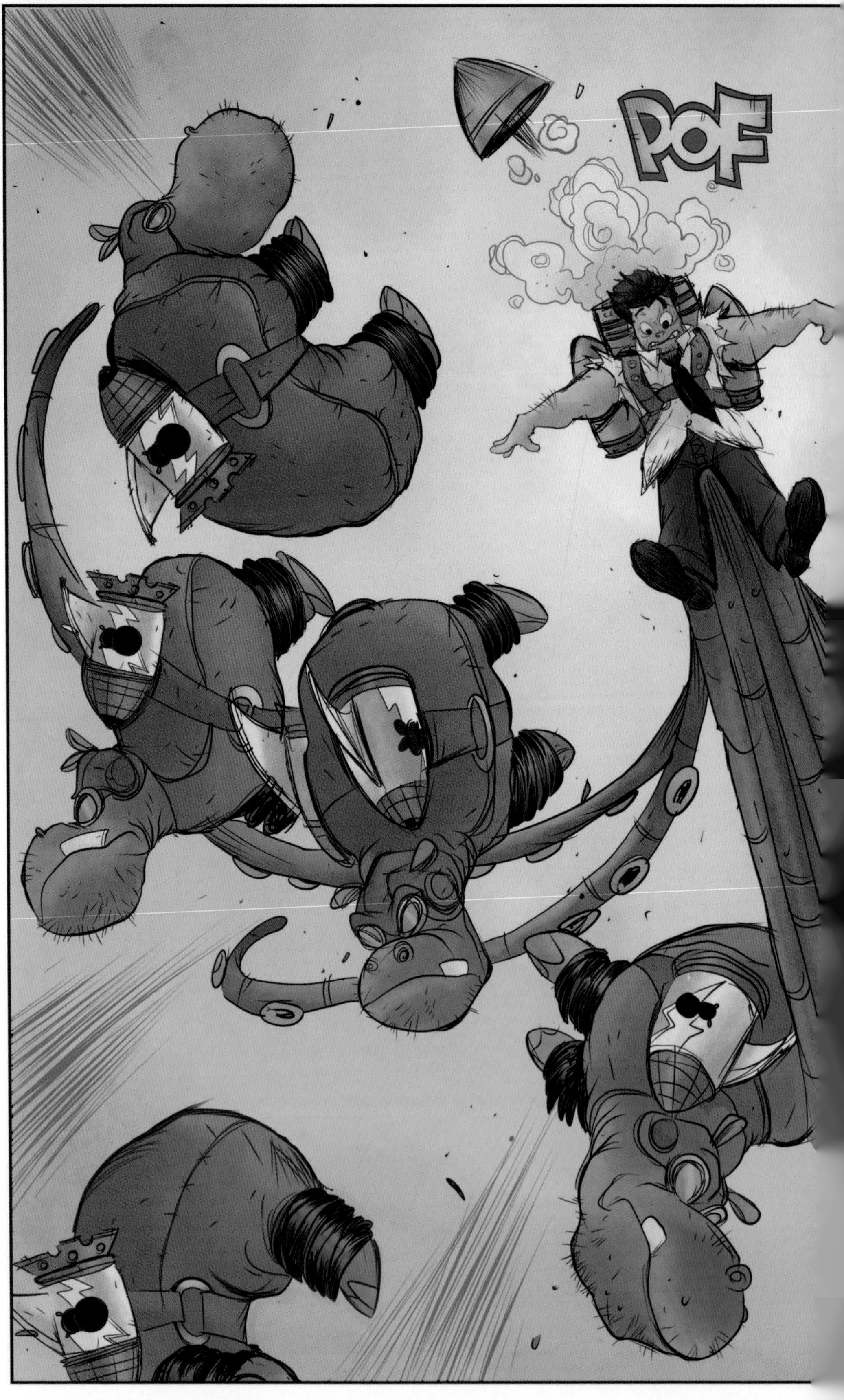
POF

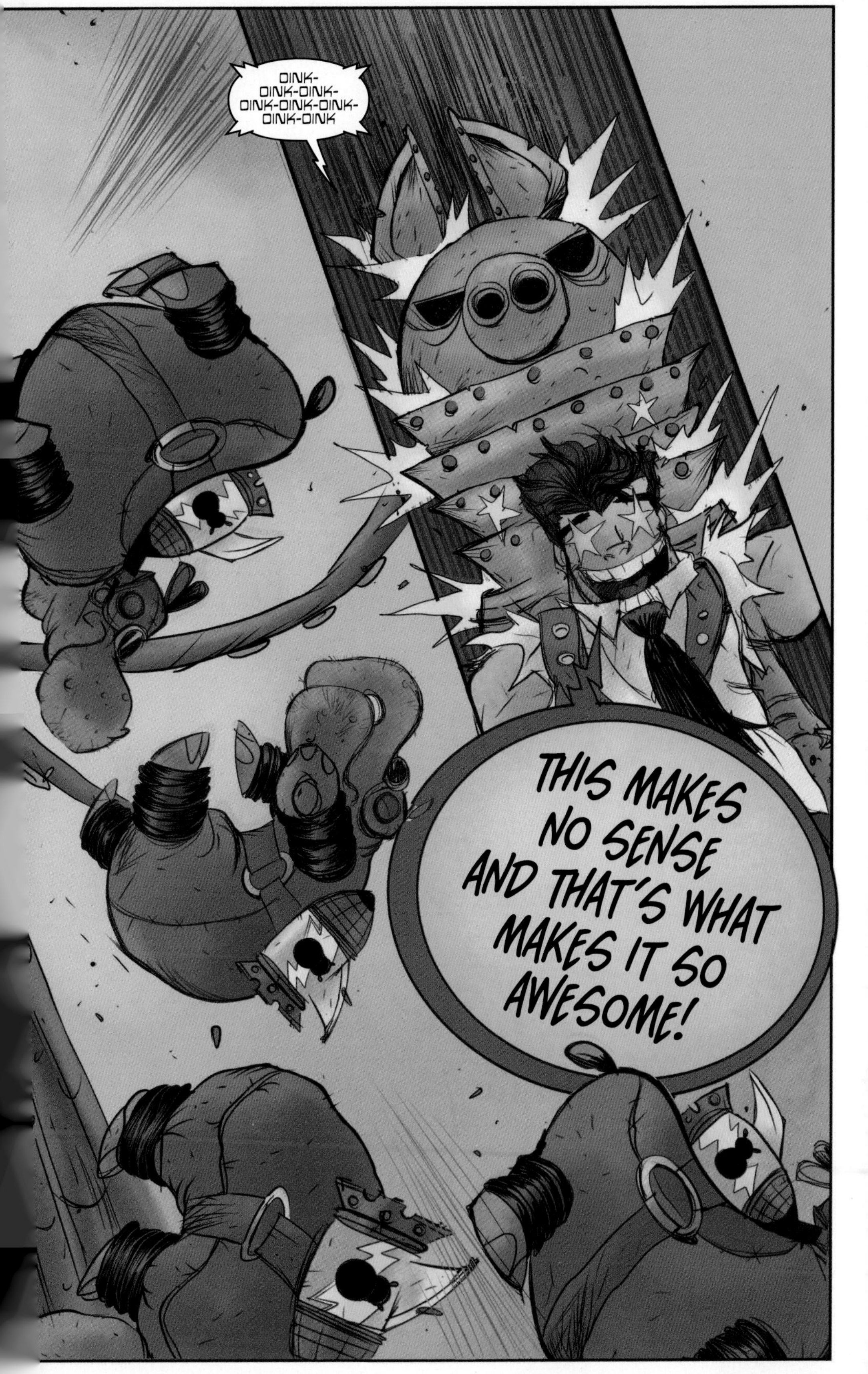
OINK-OINK-OINK-OINK-OINK-OINK-OINK-OINK
THIS MAKES NO SENSE AND THAT'S WHAT MAKES IT SO AWESOME!

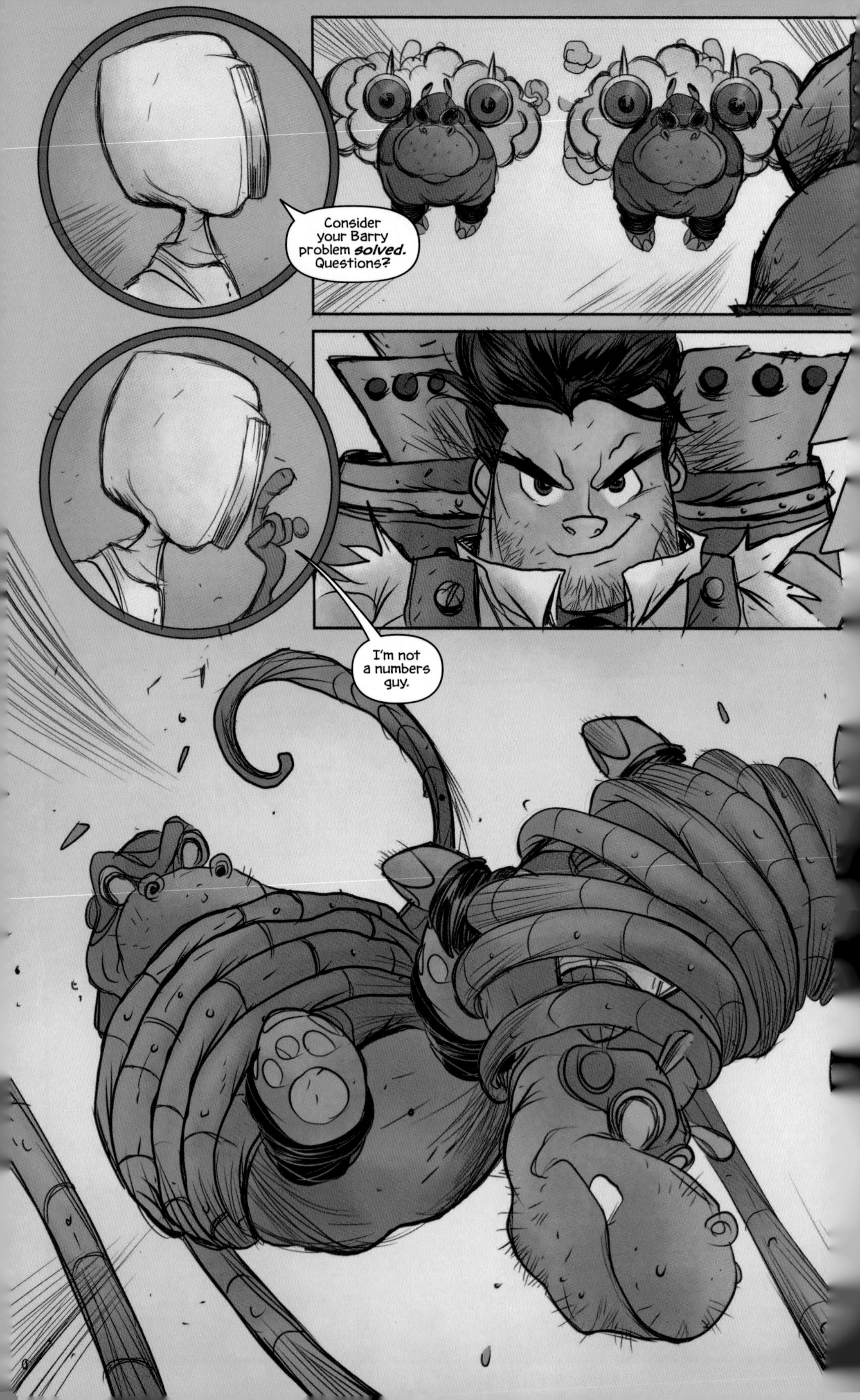
Consider your Barry problem *solved.* Questions?
I'm not a numbers guy.

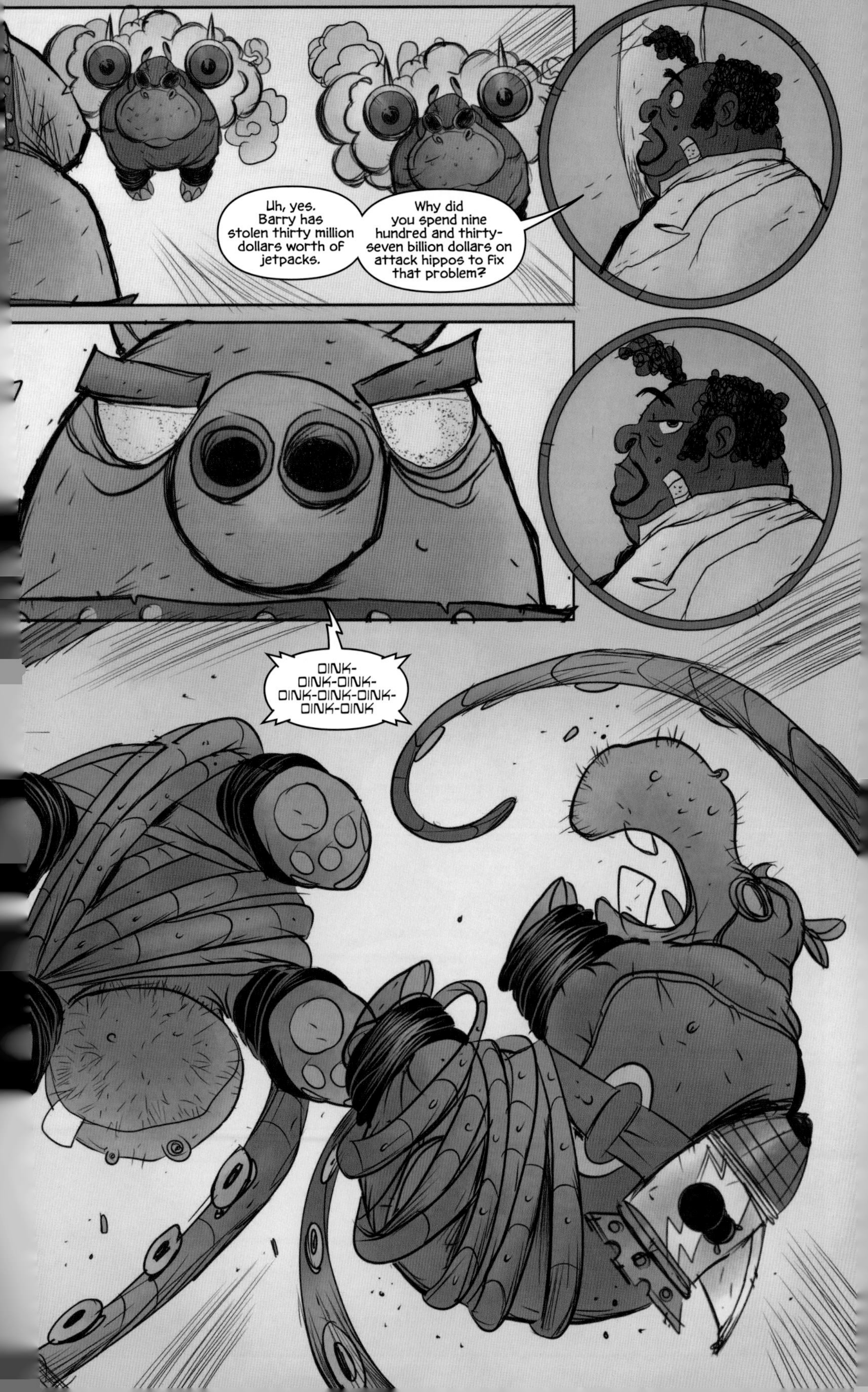

Uh, yes. Barry has stolen thirty million dollars worth of jetpacks.
Why did you spend nine hundred and thirty-seven billion dollars on attack hippos to fix that problem?
DINK-DINK-DINK-DINK-DINK-DINK-DINK-DINK

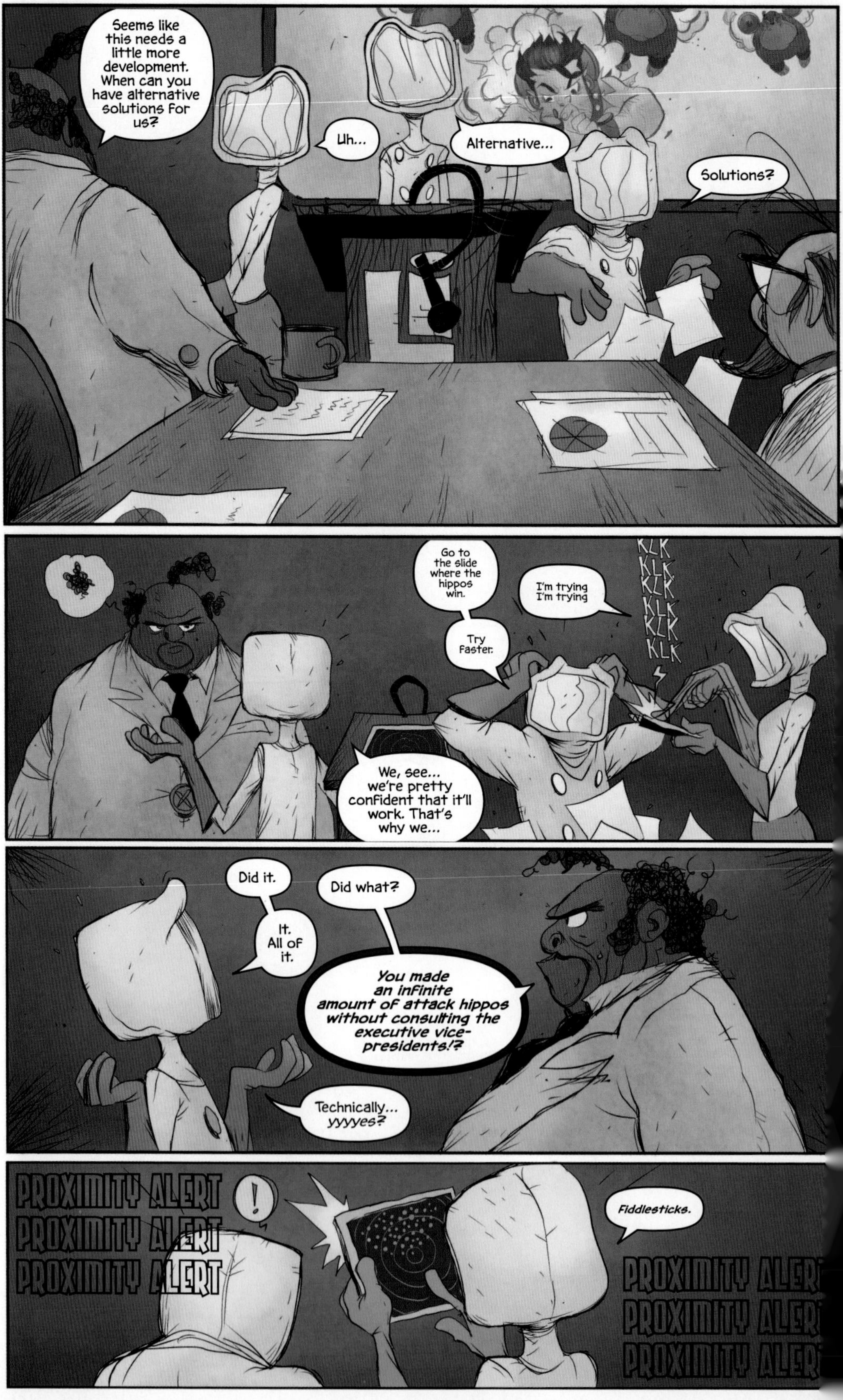
Seems like this needs a little more development. When can you have alternative solutions for us?
Uh...
Alternative...
Solutions?
Go to the slide where the hippos win.
I'm trying I'm trying
KLK KLK KLK KLK KLK KLK
Try faster.
We, see... we're pretty confident that it'll work. That's why we...
Did it.
Did what?
It. All of it.
You made an infinite amount of attack hippos without consulting the executive vice-presidents!?
Technically... yyyyes?
PROXIMITY ALERT
PROXIMITY ALERT
PROXIMITY ALERT
!
Fiddlesticks.
PROXIMITY ALER
PROXIMITY ALER
PROXIMITY ALER

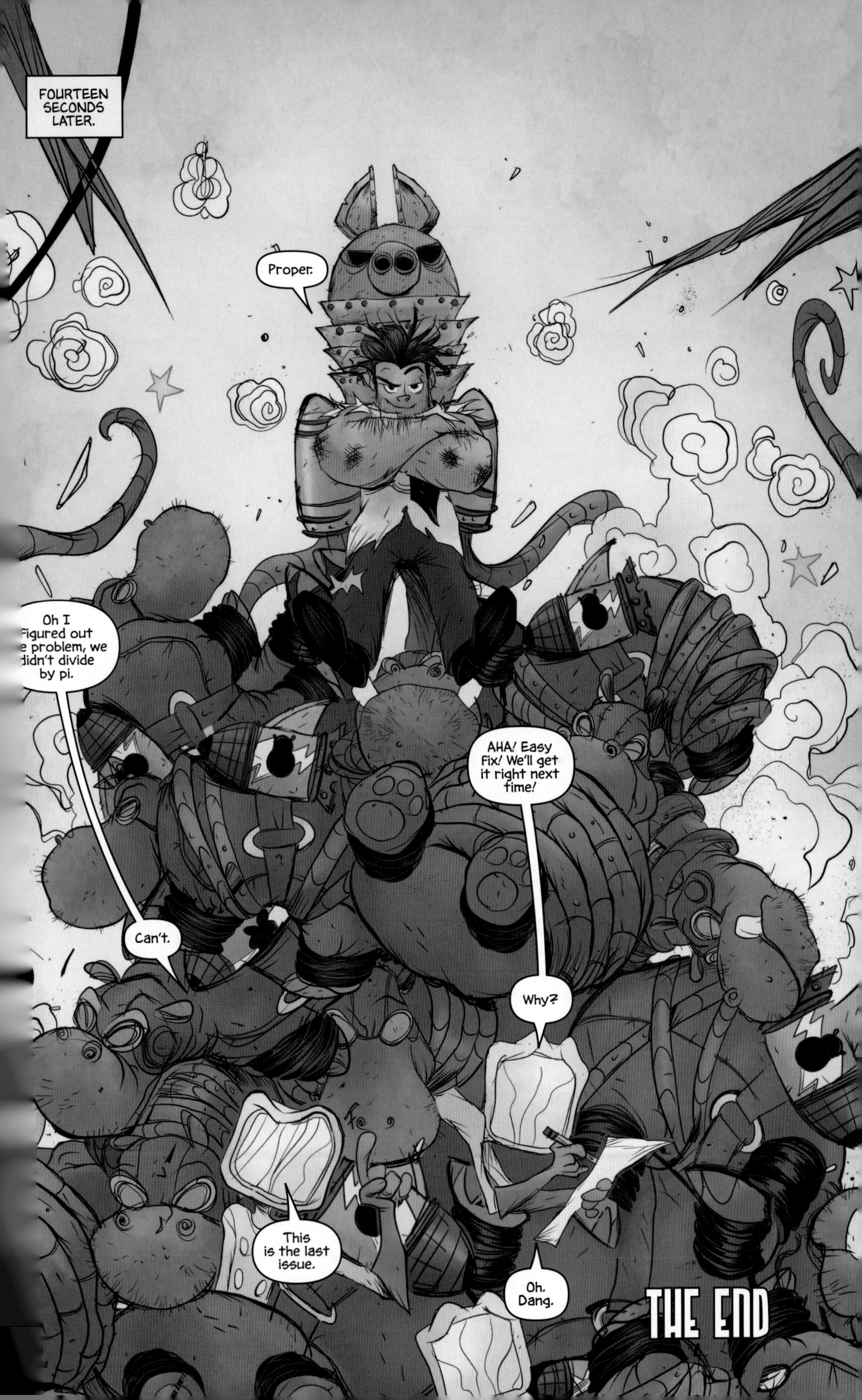
FOURTEEN SECONDS LATER.
Proper.
Oh I Figured out e problem, we didn't divide by pi.
Can't.
AHA! Easy Fix! We'll get it right next time!
Why?
This is the last issue.
Oh. Dang.
THE END

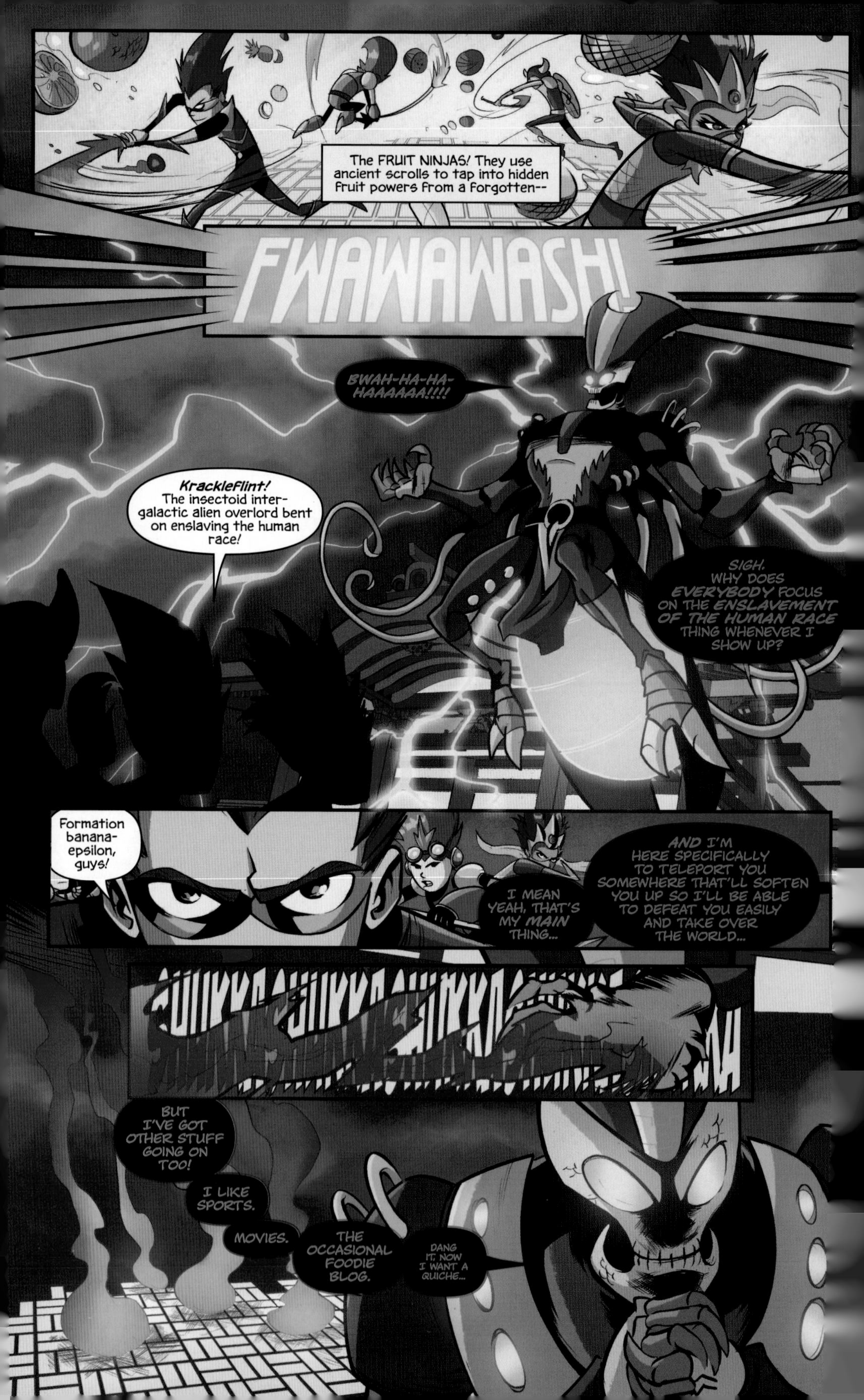

The FRUIT NINJAS! They use ancient scrolls to tap into hidden fruit powers from a forgotten--
FWAWAWASH!
BWAH-HA-HA-HAAAAAA!!!!
Krackleflint! The insectoid inter-galactic alien overlord bent on enslaving the human race!
SIGH. WHY DOES EVERYBODY FOCUS ON THE ENSLAVEMENT OF THE HUMAN RACE THING WHENEVER I SHOW UP?
Formation banana-epsilon, guys!
I MEAN YEAH, THAT'S MY MAIN THING...
AND I'M HERE SPECIFICALLY TO TELEPORT YOU SOMEWHERE THAT'LL SOFTEN YOU UP SO I'LL BE ABLE TO DEFEAT YOU EASILY AND TAKE OVER THE WORLD...
BUT I'VE GOT OTHER STUFF GOING ON TOO!
I LIKE SPORTS.
MOVIES.
THE OCCASIONAL FOODIE BLOG.
DANG IT, NOW I WANT A QUICHE...

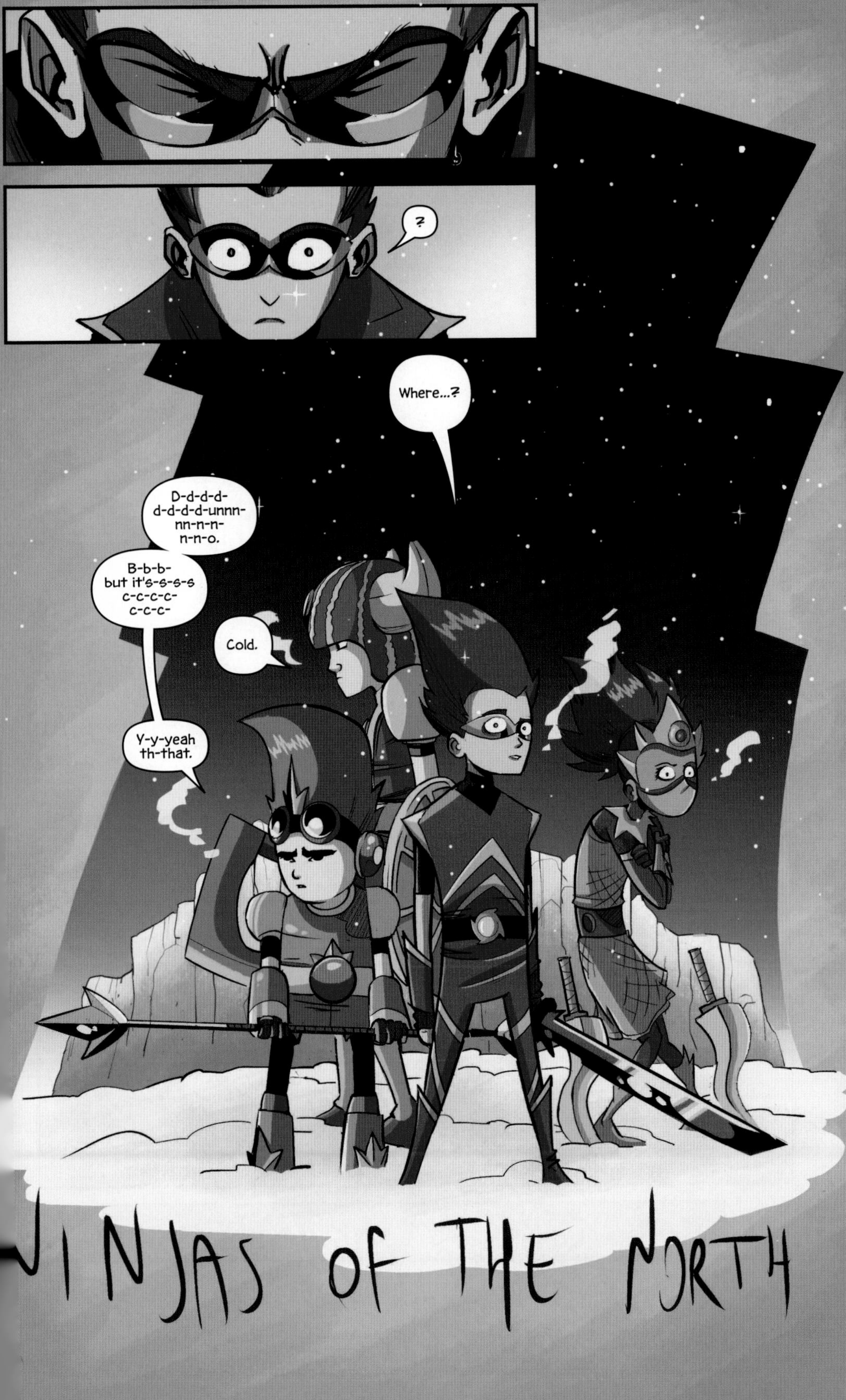
?
Where...?
D-d-d-d-
d-d-d-d-unnn-
nn-n-n-
n-n-o.
B-b-b-
but it's-s-s-s
c-c-c-c-
c-c-c-
Cold.
Y-y-yeah
th-that.
NINJAS OF THE NORTH

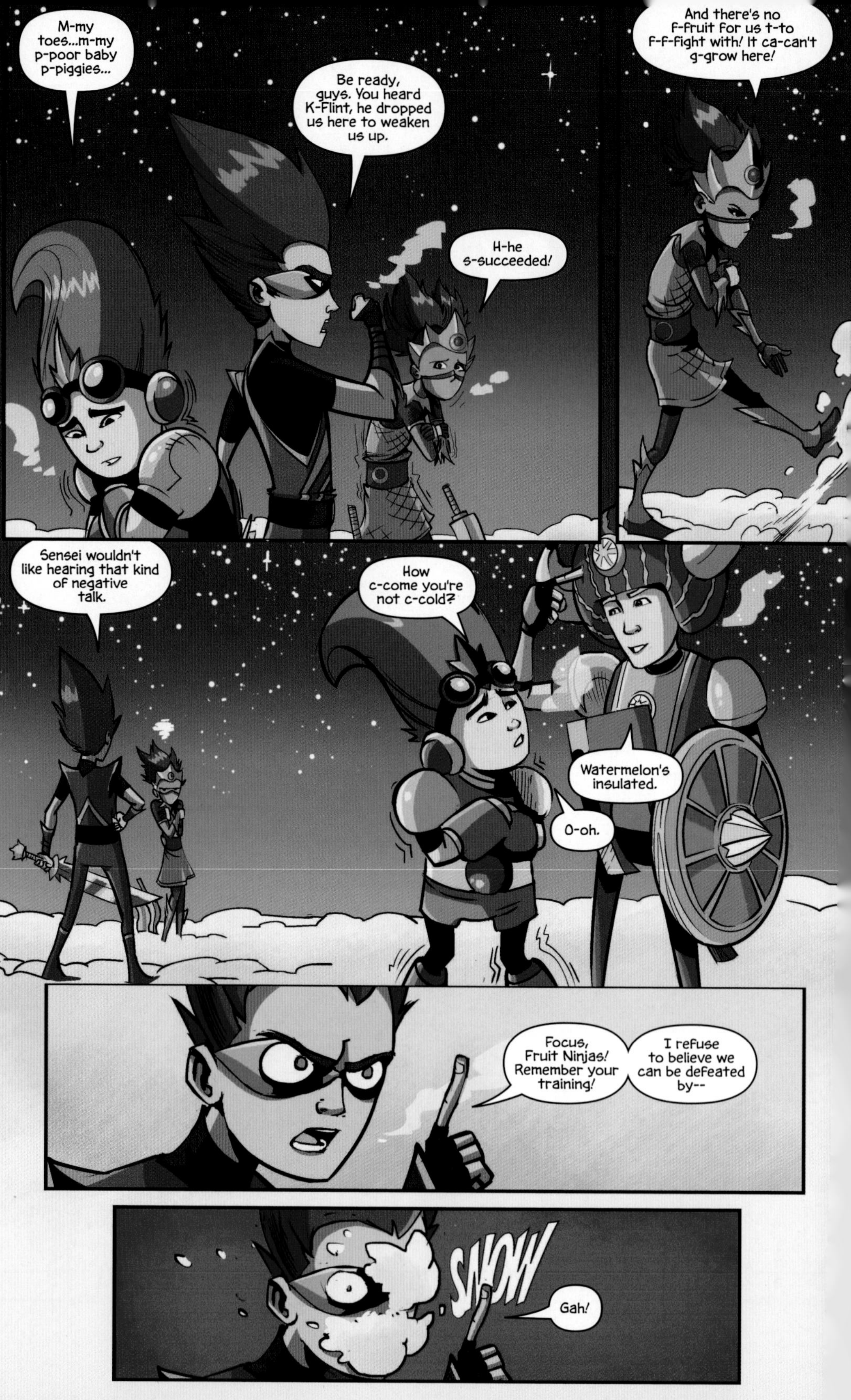
M-my toes...m-my p-poor baby p-piggies...
Be ready, guys. You heard K-Flint, he dropped us here to weaken us up.
H-he s-succeeded!
And there's no f-fruit for us t-to f-f-fight with! It ca-can't g-grow here!
Sensei wouldn't like hearing that kind of negative talk.
How c-come you're not c-cold?
Watermelon's insulated.
O-oh.
Focus, Fruit Ninjas! Remember your training!
I refuse to believe we can be defeated by--
SNOW
Gah!

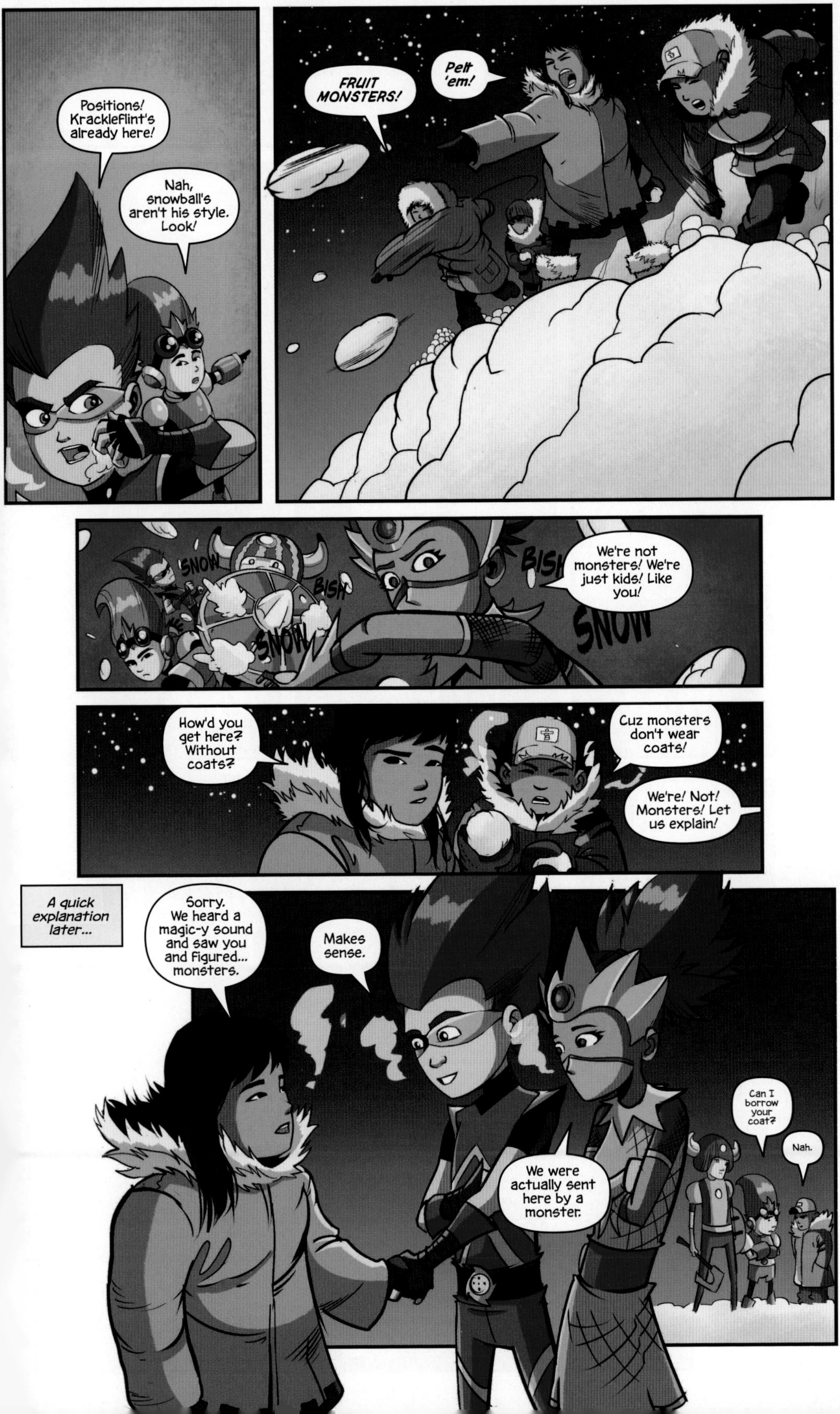
Positions! Krackleflint's already here!
Nah, snowball's aren't his style. Look!
FRUIT MONSTERS!
Pelt 'em!
SNOW
BISH
SNOW
BISH
We're not monsters! We're just kids! Like you!
SNOW
How'd you get here? Without coats?
Cuz monsters don't wear coats!
We're! Not! Monsters! Let us explain!
A quick explanation later...
Sorry. We heard a magic-y sound and saw you and figured... monsters.
Makes sense.
We were actually sent here by a monster.
Can I borrow your coat?
Nah.

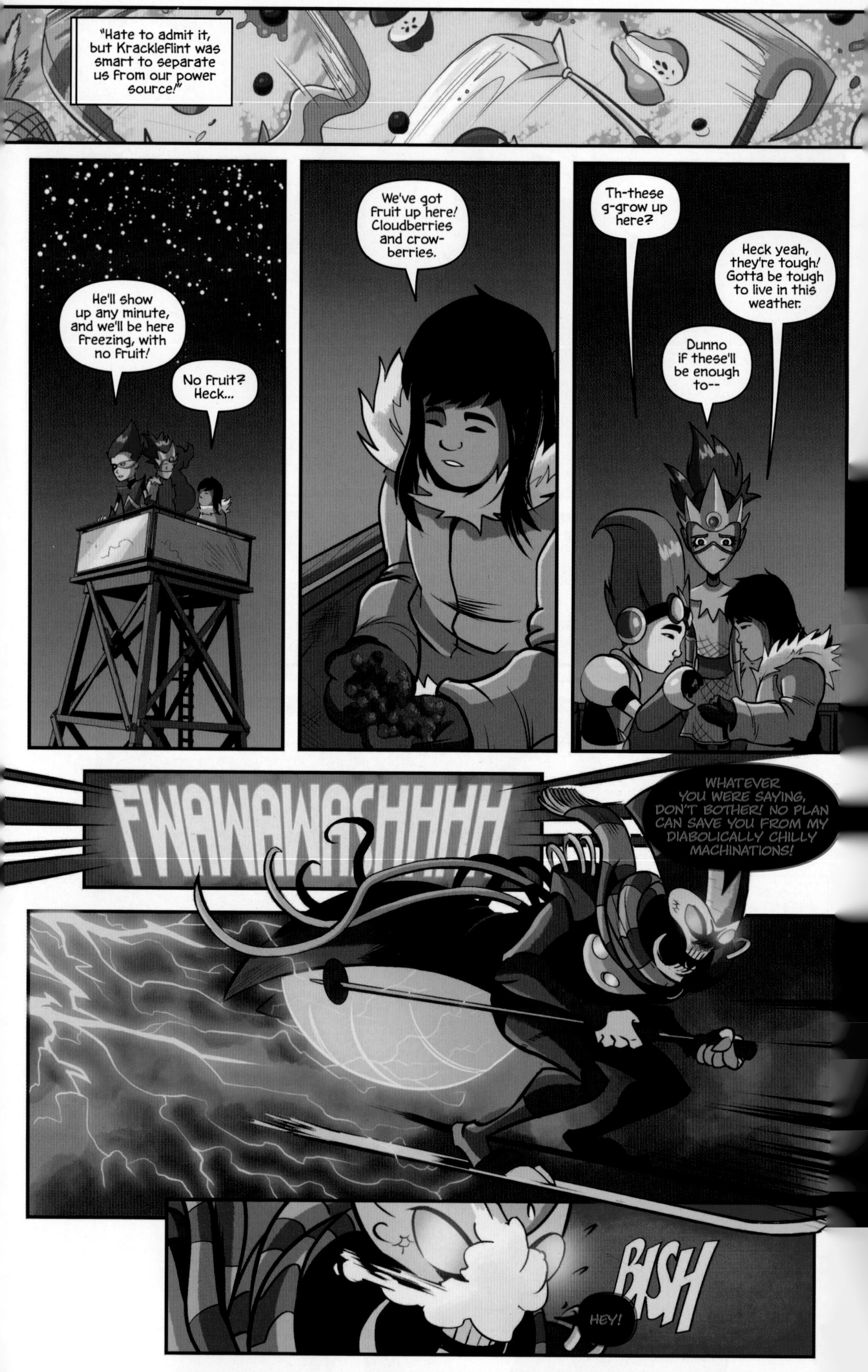
"Hate to admit it, but Krackleflint was smart to separate us from our power source!"
He'll show up any minute, and we'll be here freezing, with no fruit!
No fruit? Heck...
We've got fruit up here! Cloudberries and crow-berries.
Th-these g-grow up here?
Heck yeah, they're tough! Gotta be tough to live in this weather.
Dunno if these'll be enough to--
FWAWAWASHHHH
WHATEVER YOU WERE SAYING, DON'T BOTHER! NO PLAN CAN SAVE YOU FROM MY DIABOLICALLY CHILLY MACHINATIONS!
BASH
HEY!

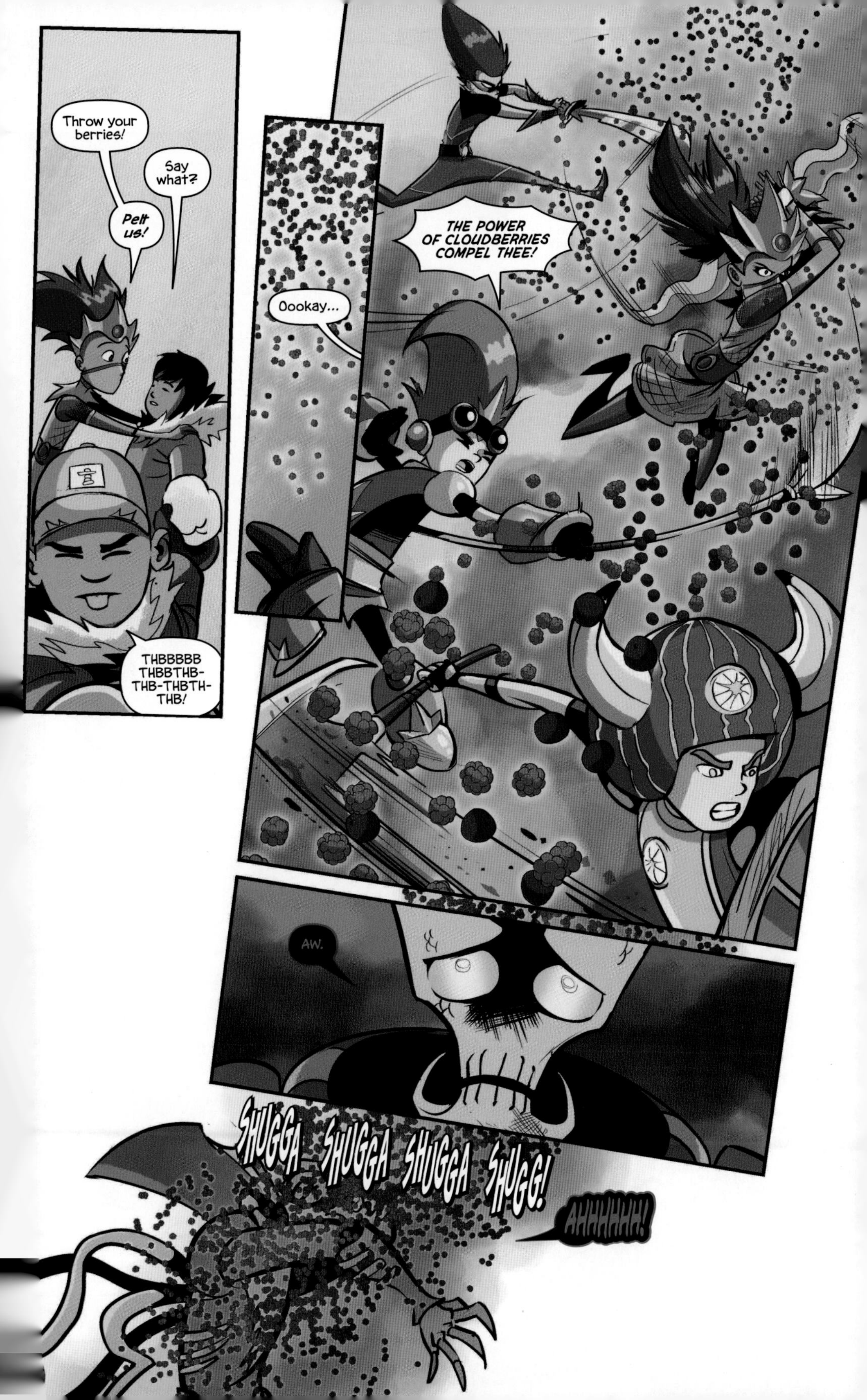

Throw your berries!
Say what?
Pelt us!
THBBBBB THBBTHB-THB-THBTH-THB!
Oookay...
THE POWER OF CLOUDBERRIES COMPEL THEE!
AW.
SHUGGA SHUGGA SHUGGA SHUGG!
AHHHHHH!

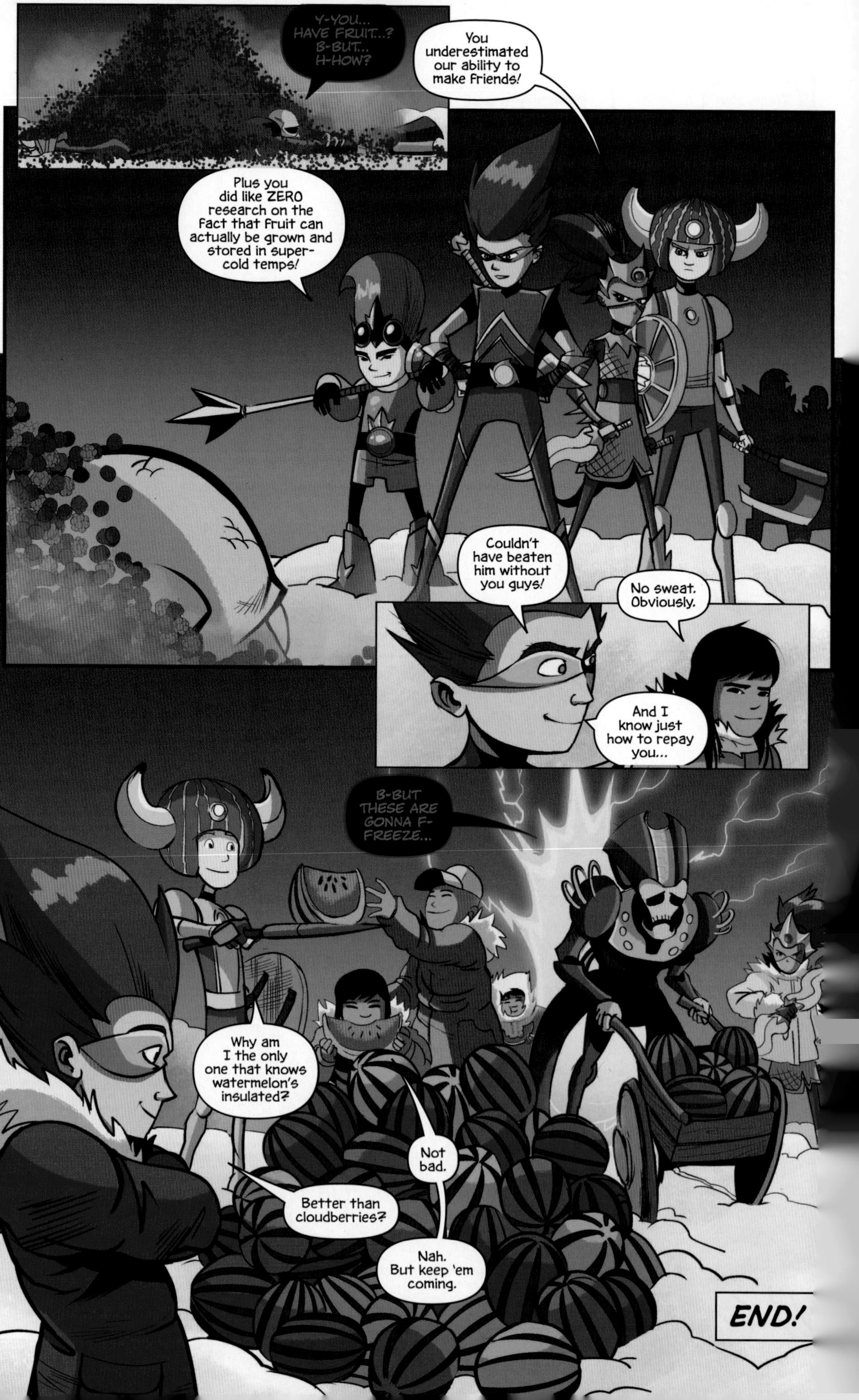
Y-YOU... HAVE FRUIT...? B-BUT... H-HOW?
You underestimated our ability to make friends!
Plus you did like ZERO research on the fact that fruit can actually be grown and stored in super-cold temps!
Couldn't have beaten him without you guys!
No sweat. Obviously.
And I know just how to repay you...
B-BUT THESE ARE GONNA F-FREEZE...
Why am I the only one that knows watermelon's insulated?
Not bad.
Better than cloudberries?
Nah. But keep 'em coming.
END!

MEET THE ANCIENT

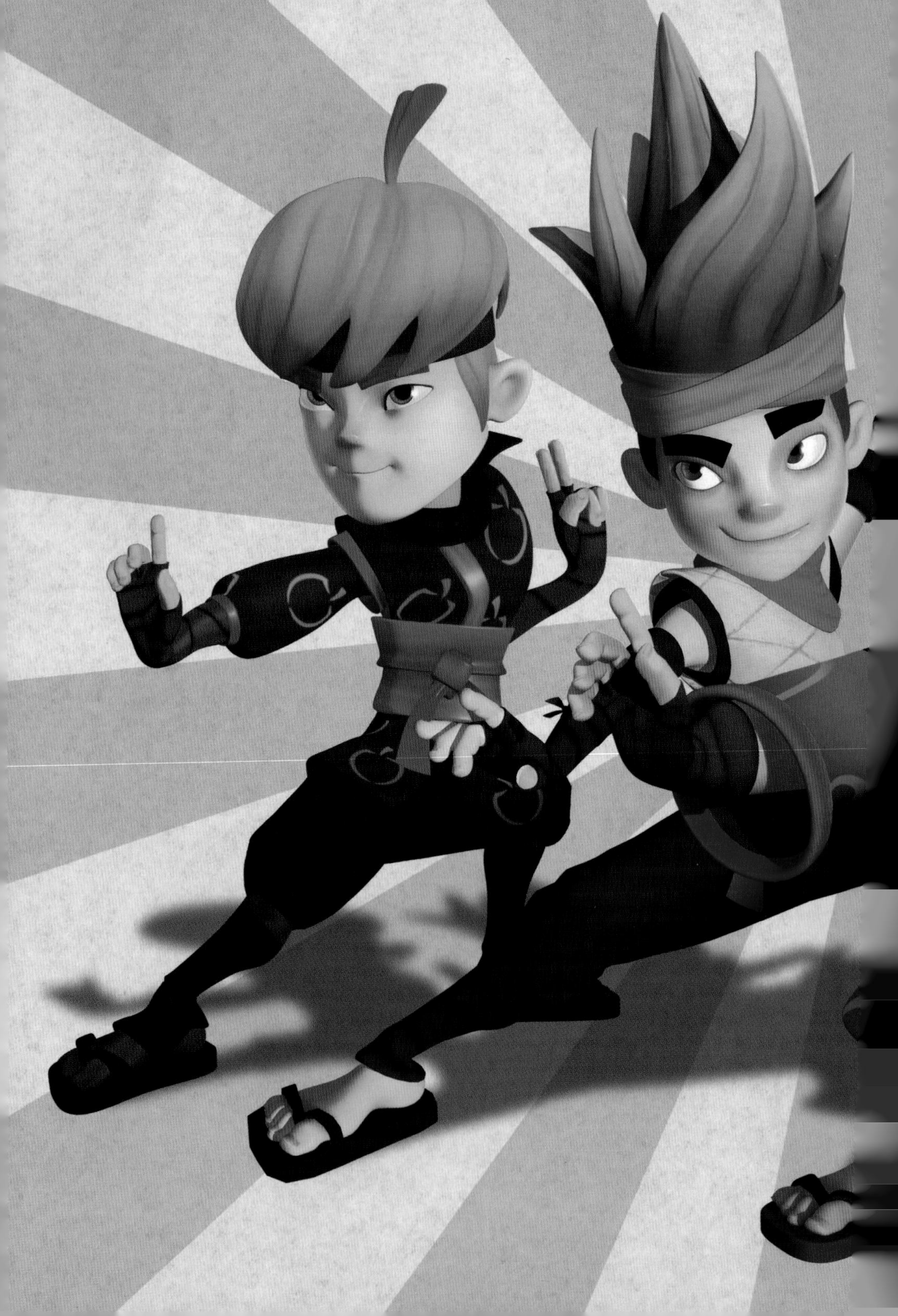

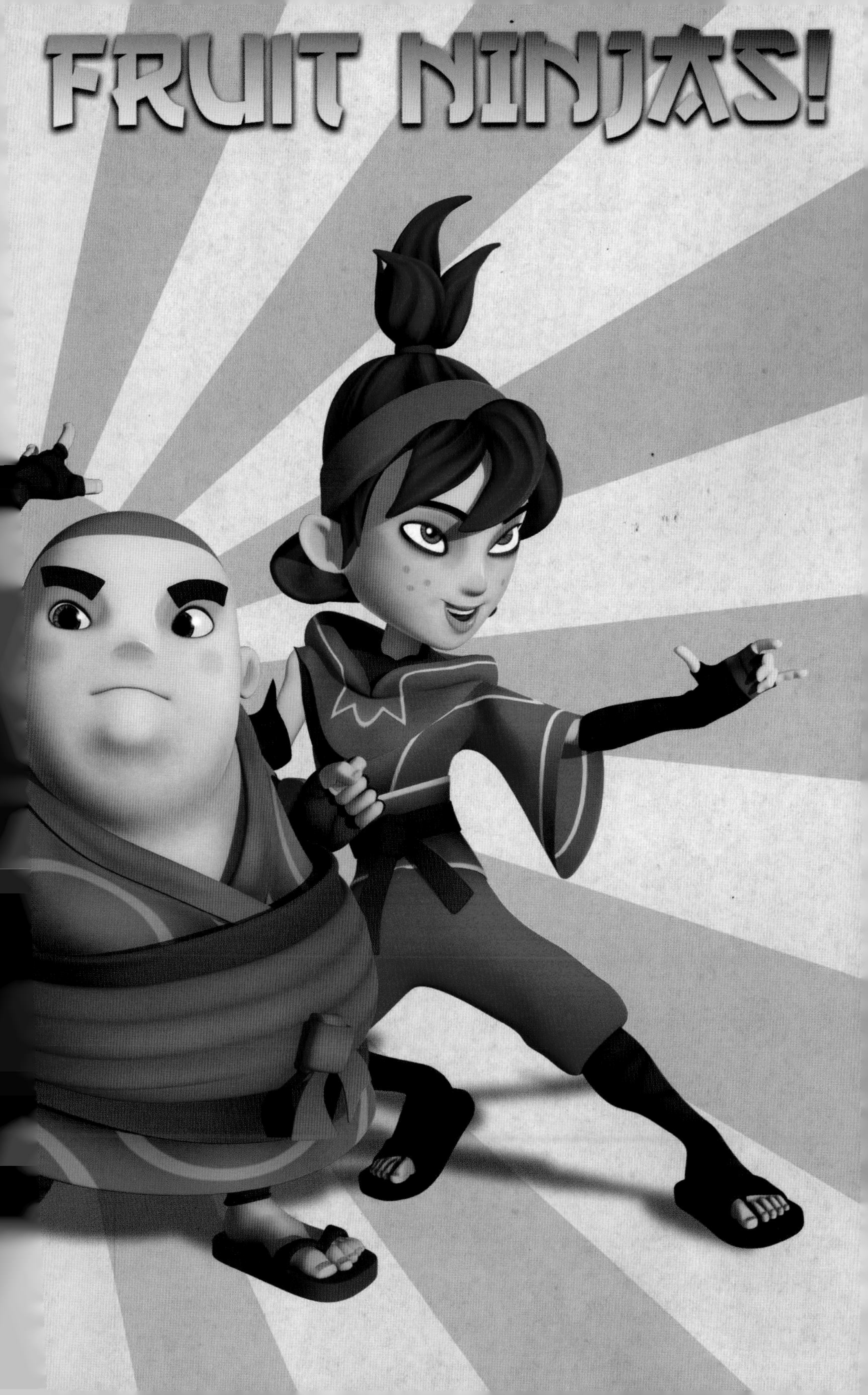
FRUIT NINJAS!

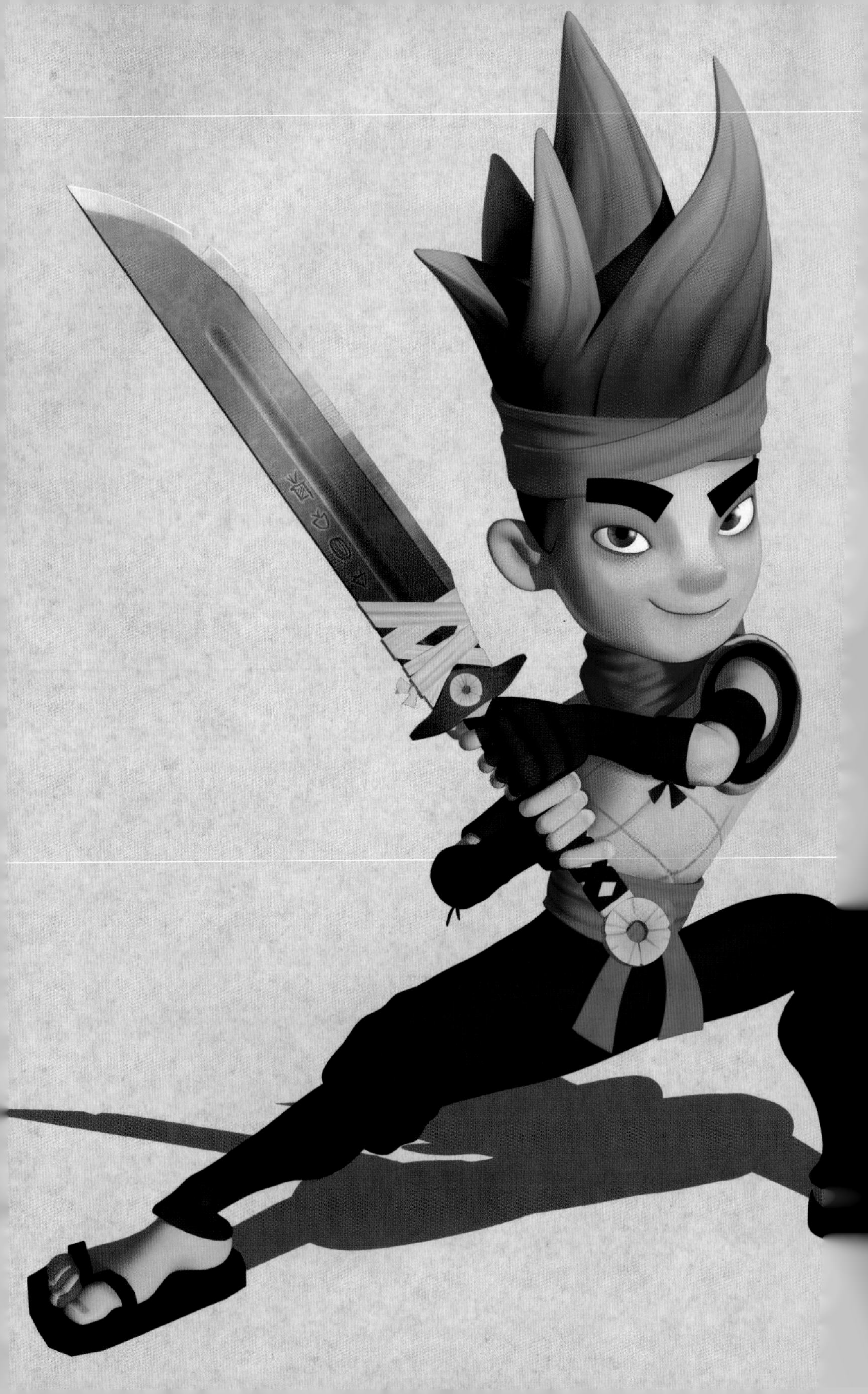

KATSURO

AGE: 14

Katsuro is his own man (despite only being 14) and the unofficial leader of his group of Ancient Fruit Ninjas. While he really isn't prepared for dojo life, somehow it seems like he's the only one who really, truly belongs there.

Originally a street urchin, Katsuro raised himself surviving on pilfered produce (a little bit Aladdin meets Sinbad with a touch of Errol Flynn thrown in). He's got street smarts, street skills, mad Parkour abilities, and he's not afraid to use them in any circumstance, from putting down the Deep Fried Samurai to putting away the dishes.

Katsuro is the embodiment of an adventurous spirit. He's a doer, gets bored easily, and can't stand sitting around. He has yet to actually learn any skills as a Fruit Ninja, rather he relies on his innate abilities and translates them to fit any situation.

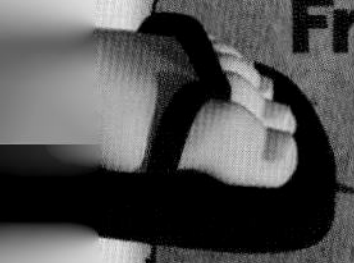

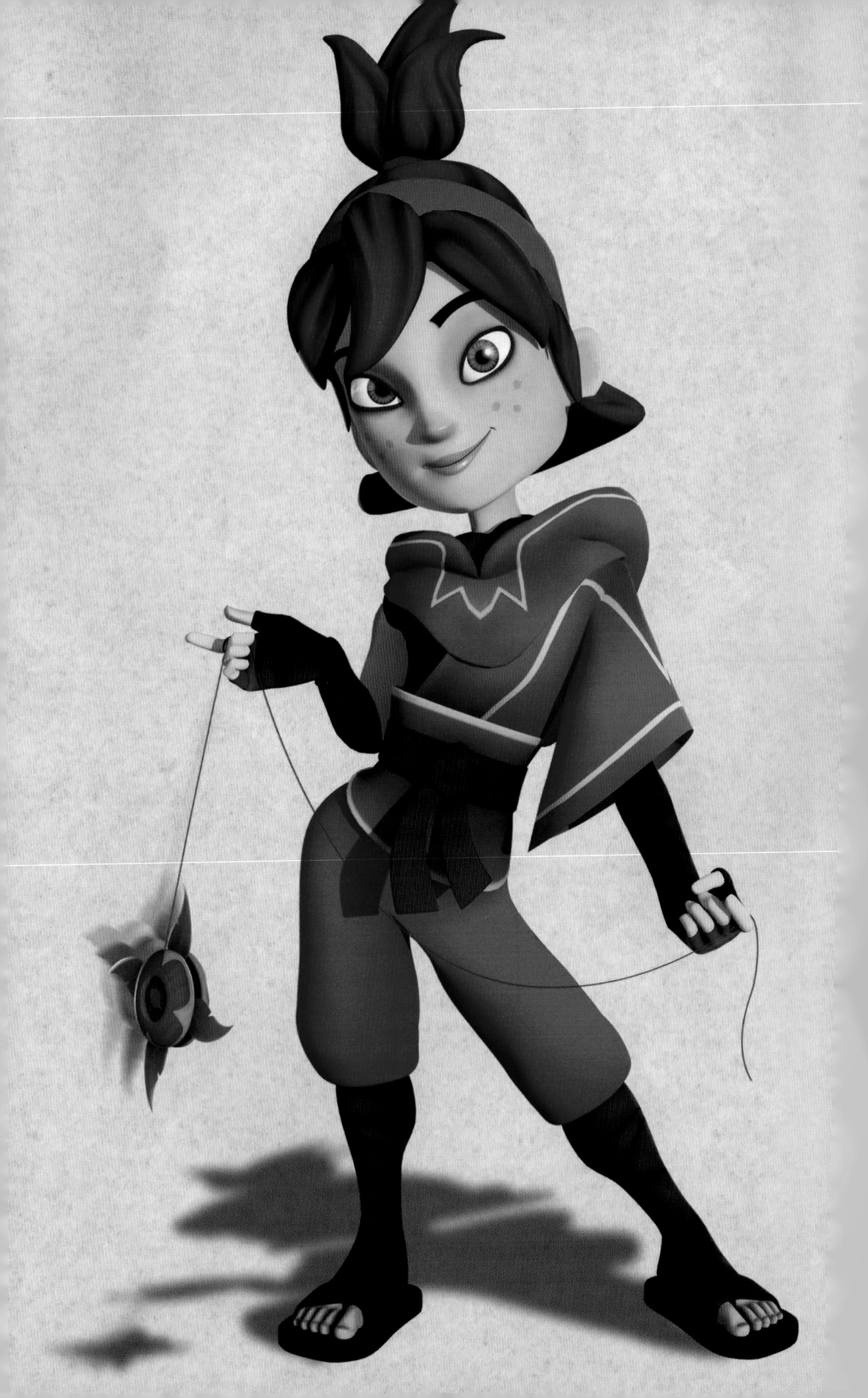

MARI

AGE: 14

Mari is the bright bulb of the group. She's' got a quick mind and an even quicker temper. Though she has read almost all the scrolls at the dojo library, she's far from bookish. She's strong willed, likes to be first in line and always fights for the upper hand.

In Mari's case, smart doesn't necessarily mean boring. She loves to laugh and enjoys her reputation as the ultimate prankster. Like a chess master, she plans her pranks very carefully, and they almost always turn out to be perfect (even though her usual target, Katsuro, might beg to differ).

Mari loves a challenge and loves challenging her teammates. She is a wonderfully good winner and an even better loser. When it comes to her fellow Fruit Ninjas, she smiles at their successes even when they overcome her best defences. Be sure not to tick her off or cheat her in any way, though. Ever seen a strawberry angry?

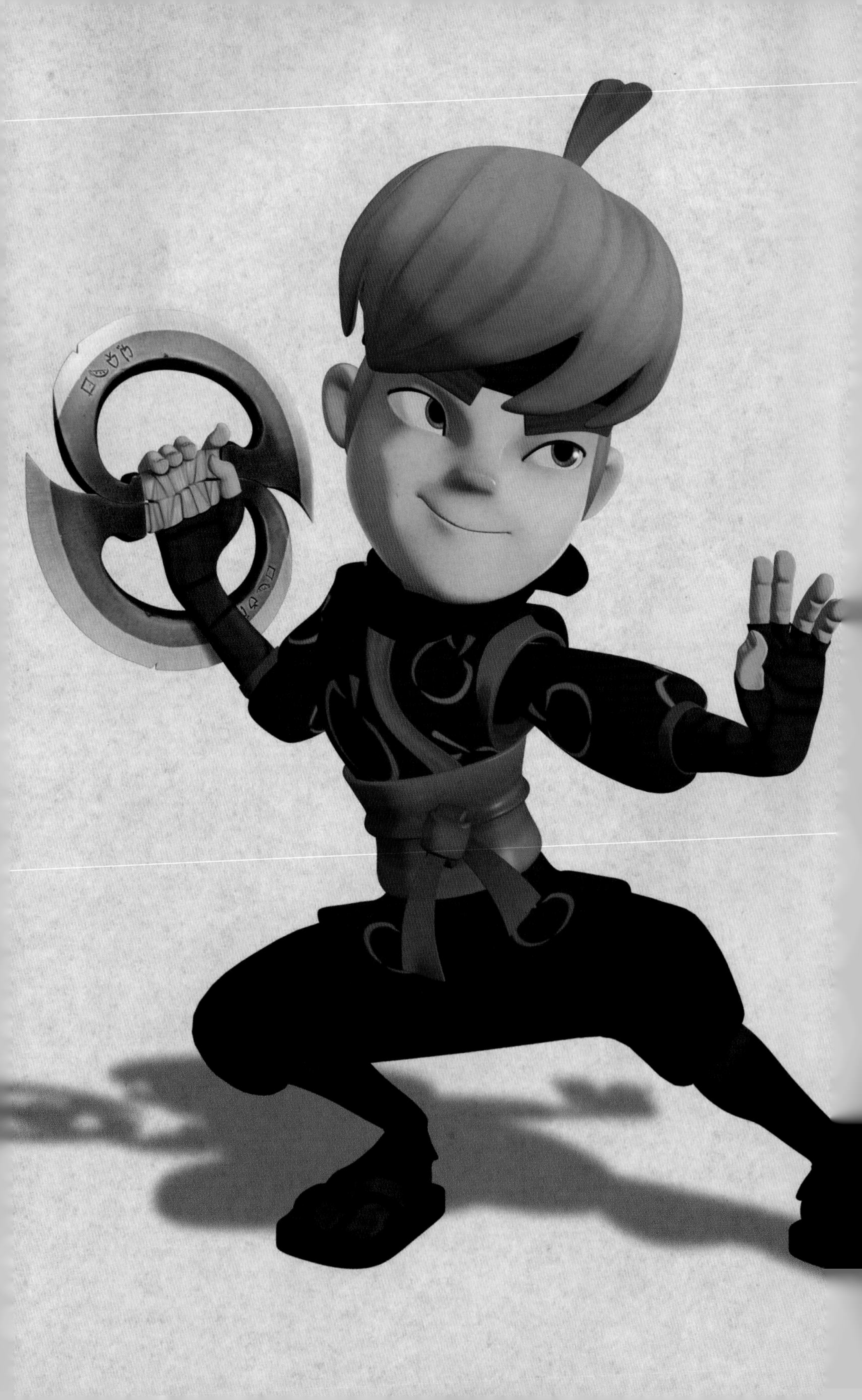

HAN

AGE: 15

The self-proclaimed, 'Sensei of cool.' While charming and chivalrous at first, Han's motives soon reveal themselves to be of the more skin-deep variety. He works hard to impress the girls and be revered or even feared by the other boys. Some say he is vain and pretentious but Han will tell you it's not his fault he was born with a heightened sense of fashion. Aside from training to be a Fruit Ninja, Han spends a great deal of time and effort trying to start new trends whether that be in fashion or some lame new 'slang' he invented.

Han's attention to detail does come in handy from coordinating battle plans right down to the 'color-blocking' of the four ninjas' wardrobe. His initial charm also serves him well in sweet-talking strangers often to the advantage of the group however the other three ninjas have to put up with a lot of whining from Han about his fruit-stained threads after every battle.

In spite of what people may believe, Han is genuine in his old fashioned chivalry. He stops to help the elderly cross the road, even when nobody is watching, and he's offended that people think he always has an ulterior motive.

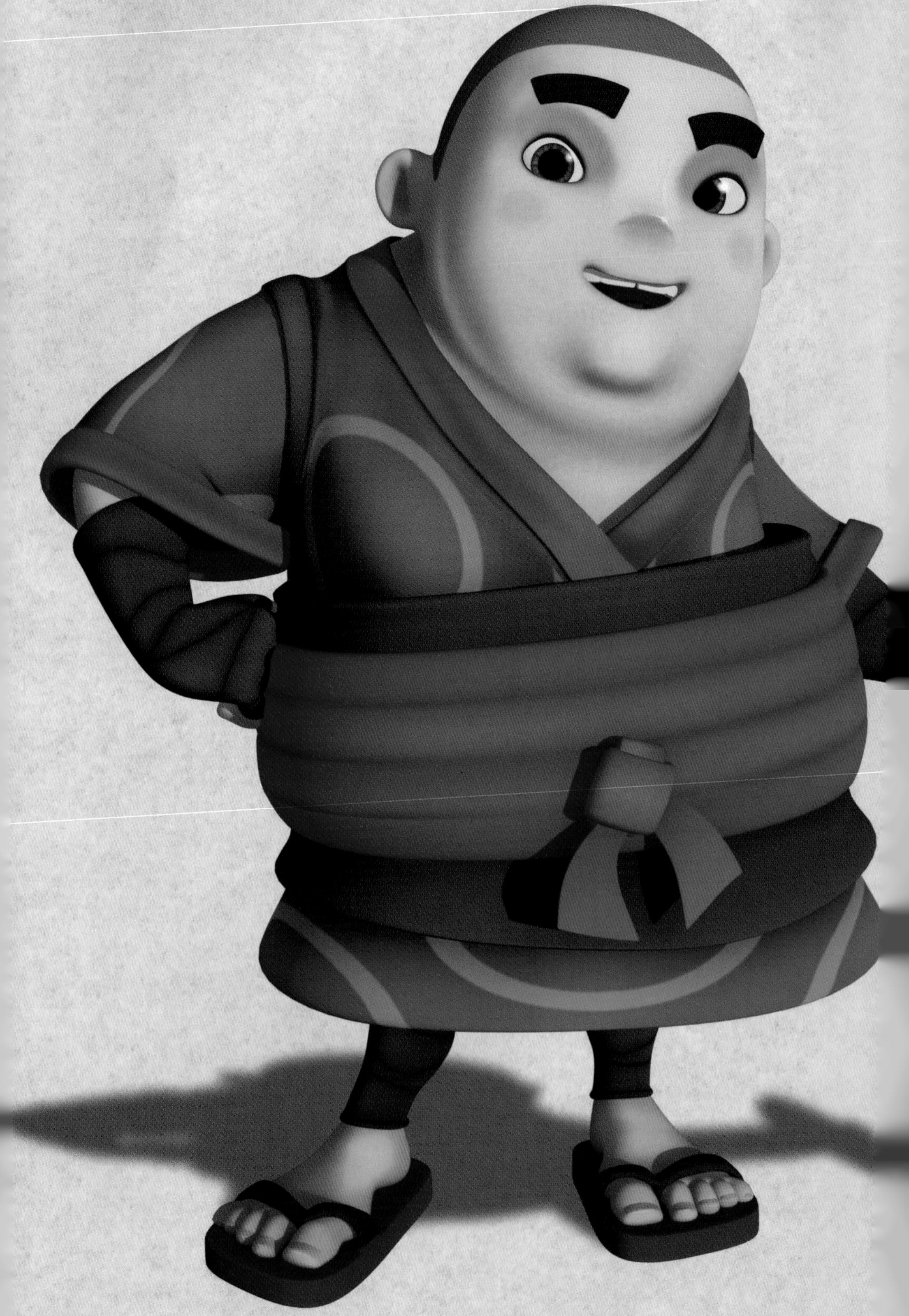

NOBU

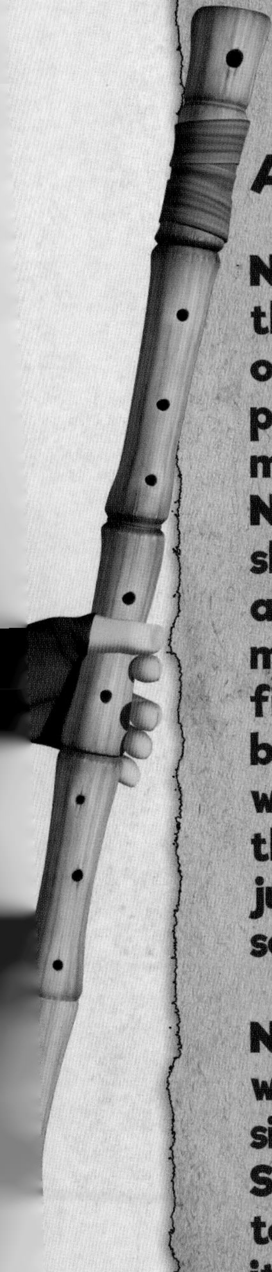

AGE: 13

Nobu is the team's spirit; the soul of the group. Ever searching for oneness with all fruit, He's kind, patient and peaceful. Though they may not be immediately apparent, Nobu possesses expertly honed ninja skills. Due to his calm nature, it takes a lot to get him riled up. Make no mistake, though, once Nobu is in fight mode, he brings it with the brute force of a thousand watermelons to the gut! He goes over the top with his moves and can fight just as well as the rest of them – sometimes better.

Nobu is not the group leader, nor would he ever think he was, but all signs point to the possibility that Sensei had planned on training Nobu to take his place one day. For Sensei, it seemed far more important that it was not the greatest of warriors that takes over, but the greatest of souls.

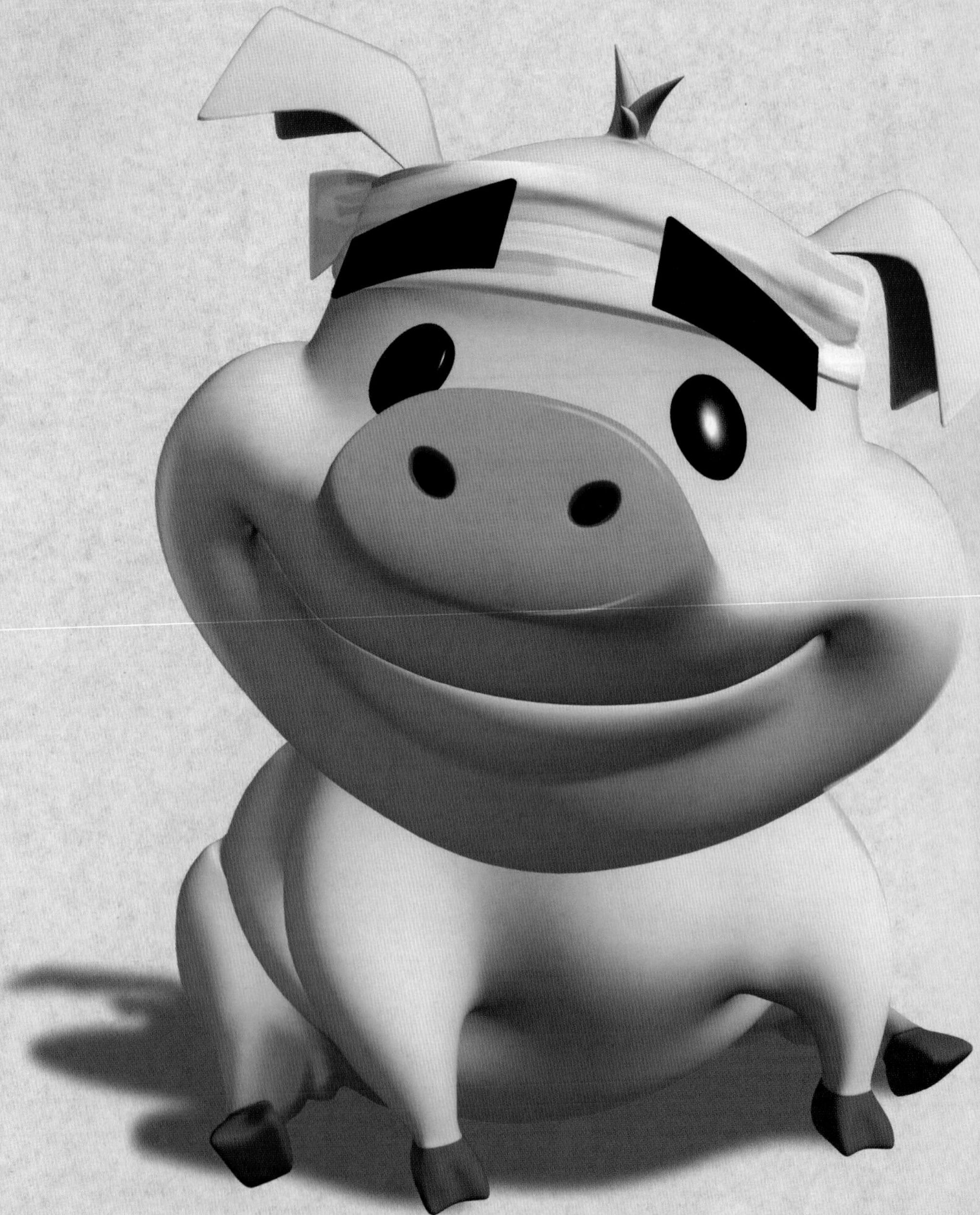

TRUFFLES

Truffles is a pig; a sweet, fun, loveable little pig that has a ton of energy and smiles to share. He doesn't talk, but he's very expressive - and hungry. He's always after a morsel of sliced fruit and his secret best friend Katsuro always finds a way to slip him something extra to eat. Both being outsiders in their own way, Katsuro and Truffles share a special bond.

Truffles dreams of being a fruit Ninja but his cloven hooves keep him from taking it to that next step. Nevertheless, he will never give up on his dream of one day becoming a real, fully-fledged Fruit Ninja!

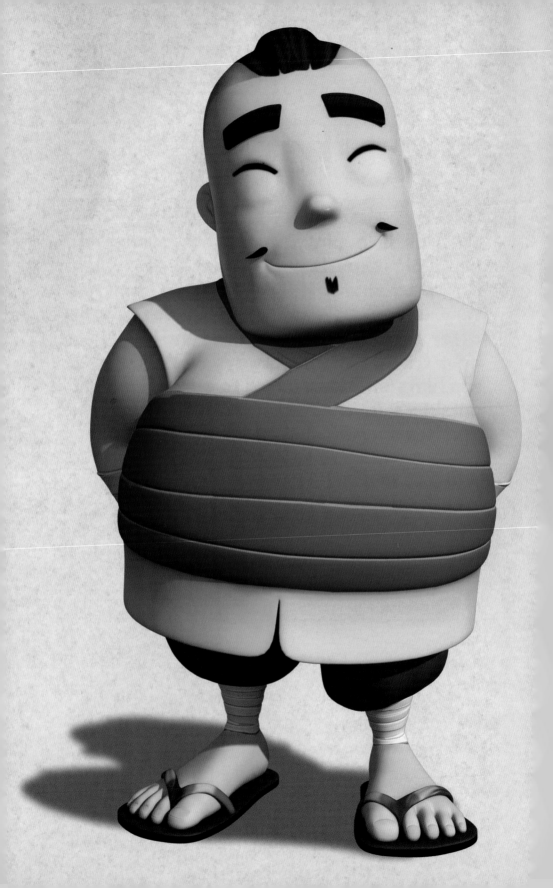

GUTSU

Nobu's uncle, local salesman and tall-tale-teller, Gutsu is a wealth of information, the vast majority of it incorrect and exaggerated. Deep down, Gutsu means well, but if he can help out and also make a profit, then all the better. His well-intended misinformation often sends the heroes on insane quests to find mysterious long lost fruits.

Gutsu doesn't know it, but Truffles is something of his ninja-pig-guardian-angel often saving his butt! If only he knew how lucky he was to have truffles watching over him.

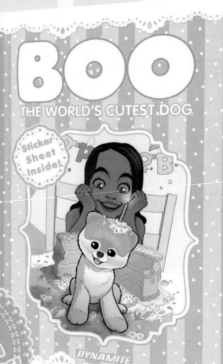